TRACKING TOM HORN'S CONFESSION

A NOVEL

GARY L. STUART

BOOK FOUR IN THE ANGUS SERIES

For information about this title or to order other books and/or
electronic media, contact the publisher:
Gleason & Wall Publishing
7000 N. 16th Street, Suite 120, PMB 470, Phoenix AZ 85020
www.garylstuart.com
gary.stuart@garylstuart.com

ISBN: 978-1-7368946-0-6 (print)
ISBN: 978-1-7368946-1-3 (eBook)

Printed in the United States of America

Cover and Interior design: 1106 Design

Other Books by Gary L. Stuart

The Ethical Trial Lawyer

The Gallup 14

Miranda—The Story of America's Right to Remain Silent

*Innocent Until Interrogated—The True Story of the
Buddhist Temple Massacre and The Tucson Four*

AIM For The Mayor—Echoes From Wounded Knee

Ten Shoes Up

Anatomy of a Confession—The Debra Milke Case

The Valles Caldera

Angus--Riding The Rio Chama

The Last Stage to Bosque Redondo

Call Him Mac

Let's Disappear

Emergence

CHAPTER 1

U.S. MARSHAL GEORGE Ramsey's office in Denver hadn't changed all that much in the four years that had passed since Angus paid his old friend a visit. The gold paint on the glass door to his office had that same chip that made George's first name look like Georg`. Once a man set foot inside, he flinched a bit at that hard smell of too many cigars, not enough fresh air through the slit-like windows, and the aroma of burnt coffee on the only coal stove allowed inside the federal building. Everybody on the third floor knew when Marshal Ramsey was in his office just from the wafting so-called aroma from his tin coffee pot boiling over on the hot stove. His window, always closed, faced east, behind his desk. Some said it was a fine mahogany desk, but you had to take it on faith on account of the corner-to-corner stacks of warrants, court filings, posters, and large brown envelopes with torn tops and blue-sheaved reports stuffed inside.

Gray had long since replaced the fire-engine red on the top of the sixty-five-year-old marshal's head. But it still curled close to his ears, and neatly slicked back to the nape of his neck. His coal-black Stetson was hanging on the rack behind his chair, just left of the U.S. flag.

"Goddamn," the marshal declared, as he stood up ramrod straight behind his swivel chair as Mrs. Ruta ushered Angus into the room. "It's been, what, ten moons since you last came up to Denver from Chama, or longer? You're looking mighty fine for a man who can't seem to keep a steady job. How 'n hell are you?"

"If you're still counting moons as a single year, George, it's been four moons. But New Mexico being civilized and all, we track the new moon every twenty-eight days. By that count I'd guess more like thirty-six moons. You're looking fit, but desk bound. How long has it been since you've mounted a fine horse and crossed a swift-running creek? Too long, I'd bet."

They traded insults with a smile for five minutes. The marshal poured his occasional deputy a tin cup of boiling hot coffee, with three sugar lumps. Each told the other his latest favorite joke, always involving a horse and a hitching rail somewhere. Ten minutes passed. They turned to the business end of this trip.

"The train trip from your Chama ranch was pleasant, I suppose, Angus?"

"Well, I prefer the gentle side-to-side sway of a long-stepping horse, but after the first half-day, I got used to the train ride jostling me. I enjoyed the scenery just fine. Is my twelve hours on a damn train why you beckoned me up here with another one of 'Your Soonest' telegrams?"

"No, it ain't. I got another job for you. And this one is a lot like that first one ten years ago. Remember the train robbers I deputized you to catch in 1890? The ones robbing the train running through the Toltec Gorge on Ten Shoes Up? That was a mighty fine piece of detective work you did, and you did it all undercover. Remember?"

"Hell yeah. But I believe it was more like 1885 or 1886. You gave me a badge, but made me stick it in my saddlebags. I hid it till I pinned it on my shirt, under my vest in the Santa Fe courthouse. You ain't thinking of doing that to me again, are you? The last two jobs allowed as how I could wear my badge on my vest. I like it that way."

"Angus, I know what you like and all, but this assignment is a short one, maybe take you four, five weeks. Six, tops. But it's real touchy. So you won't be riding up into the Iron Mountain country in Wyoming with your badge flashing in the morning sun. It's not undercover work, but it'll be better if you don't get found out by the wrong sort of cowmen. You get that stuff I sent on the Tom Horn case?"

"Yeah, I read it; four newspapers, the criminal complaint, and the case summary someone wrote up for you. But that's just a tickle, ain't it? The newspapers print what they want. The court documents only tell the legal story. And you know all that already. What would I be doing in Wyoming that ain't already been done by men who know what happened?"

"Now see. That's exactly what we want you to do. What's missing in the court papers, the newspapers, and the transcripts is the explanation for *why* the jury convicted Tom Horn of murdering that boy, Willie Nickell, when there's no damn evidence 'cept for his own damn fool confession. Even more important are the circumstances under which that damn fool confession was extracted. That's what my boss in Washington, DC, wants. And there's no one in Wyoming who is likely to tell him, or me, how 'n hell a man like Tom Horn was fool enough to confess when, if he did it, he ought to have mounted up and rode to the Dakotas. Was he tricked into making it? Was it the whiskey talking? What might make a man known for working in secret, killing at will, and getting away with it for years, open up to a deputy United States marshal? Hell, the federal government had no jurisdiction to investigate, or interrogate a man suspected of a state murder case."

"George, that's a tall order, ain't it? I don't know anything about Wyoming law, or the men I read about last week. I know all deputy U.S. marshals in the country report to the Justice Department. But you're saying the reports don't answer the *why* question—*why* Tom Horn confessed? From what I read, Tom Horn's worked as a lawman, a scout for the U.S. Army, and a range detective for the Pinkertons. He's a man who knows his job. Isn't it possible he confessed because he's guilty of killing that fourteen-year-old boy, and wants to get it off his chest?"

Marshal Ramsey swung around in his chair, got up, poked the fire in the stove, walked to the door, and asked Mrs. Ruta if she'd heard from that cow boss in Wyoming yet.

Angus could see through the open door that she was giving George the stink eye she favored when he asked her the same question too often.

"Marshal Ramsey, for the tenth time in two days, no, we have not gotten any letters, telegrams, or visits from Mr. Tommy George in Wyoming. It's spring up there, and I expect he's got cows to cut, brand, and doctor, just like my husband does down here. Do you want me to send him another telegram? Maybe he didn't get the ones you had me send him for the last five days in a row?"

"No, Mrs. Ruta," the marshal muttered, "but you tell me as soon as we get something from him, you hear?"

Turning around to face Angus sitting in front of his desk, he said, in a smoldering tone, "That woman don't take nagging near as well as she gives it out. Come on over here to the big table, I got some things you ain't seen yet."

The long pine table that covered half the room had eight straight-back cane chairs, three on each side and one at each end. Unlike the top of his desk, the surface of the table looked like a tidy accountant worked there. At the end of the table, Angus could see a stack of court files. Five thin boxes were in the center of the table. Each was about three inches deep and orderly filled with neatly clipped sheaves of paper. Large printed labels identified each box. Collectively, they painted a visual picture of the daily fare of a deputy U.S. marshal's work. OUTSTANDING WARRANTS. ARRESTS MADE. FEDERAL JUDICIAL ORDERS. STATE LAW ENFORCEMENT. PENDING ASSIGNMENTS. Four of the five boxes were full. Only the box dealing with pending assignments was empty.

"Notice anything funny about these boxes, Angus?" Marshal Ramsey asked.

"Four seem to be plumb full. One is shiny at the bottom. Tells me you're up to date on things, George, good for you."

"I am current. But the reason that one box is empty is because I had the boy from upstairs clean it out yesterday. We have a few pending things, but I wanted a clean box to show you. It's your job to fill it up. What we don't know about the

Tom Horn matter is damn important to the Justice Department. Let's talk more about that. Get yourself another cup. This is gonna take a while."

CHAPTER 2

IT TOOK MORE 'N A WHILE. Over that day and part of the next morning, Angus listened to Marshal Ramsey's second-hand understanding of who Tom Horn had been working for and why he'd been suspected in the murder of a fourteen-year-old boy named Willie Nickell. He already knew about Horn's conviction by the jury in Cheyenne. From time to time the marshal attended to other business while Angus pawed through two large boxes filled with newspaper accounts, hand-written letters to various law officers in Colorado and Wyoming, and a dozen stiff cardboard backers. Each backer was tied with string and covered a different time period. Reading them gave Angus a headache but also a mighty fine appreciation for how far and wide Tom Horn rode. There were charges, arrests, evidence, gun fights, escapes, and transcripts involving a dozen years of Tom Horn escapades in three states—Arizona, Colorado, and Wyoming. The man is a hellava story, Angus thought.

As Angus thumbed his way through the boxes, his mind kept wandering back to his wife, Jill. She was a gunsmith and the love of his life. What 'n hell am I doing so far away from her and so close to a gun hand somewhere up in Wyoming, he thought.

Horn was from Missouri, but was said to have run away from home at thirteen after a hard beating from his dad. He had a wide reputation as a man of the gun and the horse. Angus thought he and Horn probably shared the feeling of riding high ridges alone on fit horses. At sixteen, Horn had made his way to Arizona where he later hired on as a civilian scout and packer for the U.S. Army during the Apache Wars. By the mid-1880s, he held the rank of Chief of Scouts and was part of the ceremonial surrender of Geronimo. From that point to now, he was involved in range wars in Colorado and Wyoming between cattlemen and sheepmen. Along the way he was knee-deep in killing rustlers and thieves. It seemed to have started in Arizona's Aravaipa Canyon. He had a little ranch and laid a mining claim in the Deer Creek Mining District close by. Cattle rustlers got off with his entire herd, and most of his horses. He went bankrupt. From that point on he hated rustlers with a vengeance. He became a range detective and paid little account to the niceties of arrests, charges, or trials. If he caught 'em, he killed 'em.

The Pinkerton Detective Agency in Colorado took him on in late 1889. He covered a wide range in the Rocky Mountains along the Colorado-Wyoming border, working out of their Denver office. Angus knew there were two ways to look at any investigation assigned to him by a deputy U.S. marshal. One was what the record, mostly on paper, said about the details of what happened. The other was what actually happened. How and why a man got caught, or killed. One was easy to see, if you could read and remember what you'd read. The other was hard to see because it was never in print; it was always inside someone else's head. The motives and means of any criminal case had to be investigated with an open mind. Both the pile of paper and the stored memories in another man's head were important. Angus knew he could not trust the paper until he'd put boots on the ground. Otherwise it would be like imagining how smooth a Tennessee Walking Horse was before you ever threw a leg over the saddle yourself.

The reporters at several state newspapers in Colorado and Wyoming had tracked the court proceedings like buffalo hunters following a half-mile-wide trampling of earth, grass, and rock. The grim discovery of a fourteen-year old boy's body close to the gate of a barbed wire fence, three-quarters of a mile from his folk's homestead, was big news. The area was not high mountain country with soaring forests and snow-covered peaks. It was rolling hills, populated by stands of aspen, sumac, and ponderosa pines. But there was plenty of grazing meadows and valleys spread out between sagebrush and grasses of all kinds. On July 18, 1901, Freddie Nickell, Willie's ten-year old brother, found his brother's bloody body about twenty-four hours after the murder. Someone had shot him twice the day before.

Willie wore overalls, a vest, and boots. He'd been riding his father's horse on an overnight trip to the closest town. He didn't get far, a little over a mile from his house. He'd dismounted and was opening a gate when a bullet hit him below his left armpit and came out below his sternum. A second bullet blasted a hole smack in his left side, went through his intestines, and came out above his right hip. Someone walked to the body, turned him over on his back, and pulled his shirt open. He placed a rock under the boy's head. His father, working in the barn at his ranch, heard the shots but thought someone was out hunting. There were several family ranches within a few miles and hunting was common. When Willie did not come home that night, they guessed he'd stayed in town. Nothing unusual about that. Freddie had chores to do up that road the next morning; he'd found his brother's body and rode back to the house at breakneck speed, screaming, "Willie is murdered!" all the way.

Four days later, on July 22, 1901, a coroner's inquest was convened in Cheyenne, the Laramie County seat. Several witnesses were called, but nothing determinative was learned, so the inquest was adjourned, subject to later call. On July 23rd, when the inquest reconvened, Tom Horn was called as a witness. Before his testimony, there was nothing for him to fear. His ill-advised speeches and his penchant for volunteering information not asked about by the county prosecutor changed the tone and risk of the coroner's inquest. Five months later, on December 26, 1901, the coroner's jury issued a bland statement. "We the jury empaneled to inquire into the death of Willie Nickell, find that the deceased came to his death on July 18th, from a gunshot wound inflicted by a party or parties unknown."

Tom Horn was a suspect because his job was to deal with cattle rustlers and make life hard for sheepmen. He was also suspected because of his answers at the inquest. But there was no hard evidence, other than the fact that he was in the area. That was not enough to arrest or charge him with anything.

Eighteen days after the coroner's inquest was closed for lack of evidence, on January 13, 1902, the Laramie County Sheriff arrested Tom Horn for the murder of Willie Nickell. On January 23, they gave him a preliminary hearing. The surprise witness at the hearing was a deputy U.S. marshal named Joe LeFors. LeFors testified for two days. He told Judge Samuel Becker that Horn had confessed to killing the boy. He said the confession was "overheard" by Deputy County Sheriff Les Snow, and court reporter Charles Ohnhaus, from the room next door. Mr. Ohnhaus had taken down the confession, word for word. Snow and Ohnhaus also testified and confirmed LeFors's surprise testimony. Horn's defense lawyer asked for bail. Walter Stoll, the U.S. Attorney for Wyoming, and also Laramie County prosecutor, argued that the proof against Horn, his confession, was evident. He said the presumption of guilt was great. The judge bound Horn over for trial.

It took a tad over three hours for Angus to get the facts on paper straight in his head. His stomach was pumping some, but his head was telling him something was wrong with the paper. He asked Marshal Ramsey for the straight of it.

"So, Angus, here's your assignment. The Department of Justice in Washington, DC, wants us to find out what really happened up there in Wyoming in those eighteen days. Why in tarnation was a deputy U.S. marshal even involved? How did he get Horn to confess? How come a county deputy sheriff just happened to be close by, in the next room? Did they know Horn was going to confess? Is that why a court stenographer was there taking notes? You need to get yourself up there and find the answers for us. But you won't be alone on this. A man working for the U.S. Attorney of Colorado, somewhat undercover like you, named Tommy George will partner with you on this. You work with him. The two of you need to find out what really happened and get it down in writing. Come back down here as soon as you can so we can both report to Washington, DC. They want answers."

CHAPTER 3

ANGUS'S FIRST MEETING with Tommy George was straight-
forward. They took one another's measure. Is he a man of
the horse, or a storekeeper? Can I trust him? Has he got the
makins'?

Angus was sitting in the big overstuffed chair in the lobby
of the Brown Palace Hotel when Marshal Ramsey walked in,
with Tommy in stride. They spotted him from forty feet away
and swung toward him, like a well-trained team of buggy
horses. Angus thought Tommy George walked like a horseman should—not feeling comfortable so close to the ground.
He looked forty, but Angus remembered being told he was
about thirty, maybe. He was lean, looked thoughtful, and had
a round face broken into strips of wrinkled skin running up
and down from side burn to chin and across the lower half of
his face. His hazel eyes, from ten feet away, were ablaze with
curiosity, but almost lost under a light brown tangle of eyebrows. He looked steady, the way a horseman had to be—at a
long trot, or in full gallop. He was a man not to be trifled with.

As Tommy George strode across the carpeted lobby toward Angus, he felt comfortable being herded toward a man in a black, wide brim hat that looked like it'd seen more than one winter storm, weathered, but still upright. In Tommy's world, most men rolled out of their bunks at the brink of dawn and put their hats on. Mostly, they kept their hats snugged, or loose depending on the kind of cow work being done till nightfall.

Both men had faces confirming a lifetime outside. They had the bearing and gait of men who knew exactly where they were going, even if they'd never been in this draw or creek bed before. They trusted their instincts about things within their line of sight, but were always wary of things either out of sight, or out of mind.

Marshal Ramsey did the introductions.

"Angus, this is the man from Wyoming I told you about. He knows the Laramie River and Iron Mountain area like you know the Chama River and the Toltec George."

"Howdy, Angus," Tommy said, offering not just his hand, but a nod of the head, and a small smile.

Angus returned the smile, the nod, and extended his hand. Anticipating a cast iron grip, he pushed his hand deep into Tommy's outstretched right palm. There was no shake to this handshake. They gripped down well into the notch between thumb and first finger and took stock the way men with outside work always do. Neither flinched; both squeezed without the other taking notice, and both relaxed the grip simultaneously as though it'd been choreographed.

"Good to meet you, Tommy. I hear you're a man that can ride six hours at a long trot as long as your horse's got water and feed along the way."

"I can most always stay in the saddle for twenty miles or so, but it sometimes depends on whether I had two tin cups of coffee, or just a long swallow of water. Nature's calls sometimes interrupt a long stay in the saddle."

As so, with just a few words, a handgrip, and a deep look into the set of one another's eyes, Angus and Tommy established a trust that would benefit both in the job ahead. Marshal Ramsey had booked a corner table at the dining room at the Brown Palace, a ten-year-old six-story hotel in the heart of Denver. They headed that way without further talk. These were not men who carried on a conversation while walking across a public room.

The three men ate with their hats on, holding the knife in their right hands, forks in the other, and nods of agreement as to what Marshal Ramsey wanted from them. They were to ride soft and easy and let the Wyoming lawmen do their job. They were not to try and solve the whole case or interfere with it in any way. Their job was to figure out that damn confession. If it was as true as the Wyoming lawmen said it was, then he'd face the noose in Cheyenne. And the Colorado case might never come to trial. But if the law up there tricked Tom Horn, then maybe a different outcome was in order. They left the dinner table with full stomachs, toothpicks at hand, and a job to do.

CHAPTER 4

THE COLORADO ATTORNEY general's Office had seen better days. It was on the second floor of the capitol building
on Colfax Avenue in Denver. When Tommy George first saw
it that cold winter day in 1902, he thought it looked familiar. He was a block away in what Denver called a horse cab.
Pulled by a team of draft horses and driven by a man who
looked like he might die before they trotted that last block
to the familiar-looking building, the cab was yellow and had
three leather seats. The man, wearing a seaman's black cap,
coughed and shook something awful. From two blocks away,
the building reminded Tommy of pictures he'd seen in high
school in Laramie of the U.S. Capitol Building in Washington.
He would soon learn why he had that feeling. It was built to be
intentionally reminiscent of the United States capitol. Built out
of Colorado white granite, the distinctive dome was covered in
copper panels. Just six years later the panels would be gilded
with gold leaf from a Colorado mine—to commemorate the
Colorado Gold Rush.

The Colorado territory was established in 1861 on the cusp of the Civil War. The bustling territory won statehood in 1876. Its Constitution established the Office of the Colorado attorney general as one of four independently elected statewide offices. Craig Addis Blakey was the chief deputy attorney general. Friends called him Addis. Some said he'd been a fine lawyer before serving a term as a state judge. He got the election bug and ran for attorney general against Charles C. Post in 1900. Post beat him handily, which caused Addis to become known as 'pert near AG. But Post recognized talent and offered Addis the job of chief deputy. By 1900 there were 540,000 people in Colorado. Most of the economic action had shifted from the silver mines in Leadville to the gold fields around Cripple Creek.

Addis had deputized Tommy George as a part-time investigator looking into various criminal activities taking place along the border between Wyoming and Colorado. Like Angus, Tommy had done his work by keeping his badge in his saddlebags. He'd earned his pay by rooting out several escapees from the Colorado State Penitentiary just east of Cañon City, Colorado. Built in 1871, it was largely known for being the home of Colorado's death row.

Wyoming seemed safe to escapees from Cañon City, because county sheriffs in Colorado never crossed the state line into Wyoming. Tommy George never paid any mind to the border. When he was asked to track down an escapee, he crisscrossed the border till he found his man. He bound him up and delivered him to Cañon City, sometimes strapped to a pack mule. Addis favored mules for jobs such as rounding up warrant busters and escaped prisoners.

"Tommy George, you are no taller now than you were two years ago when I last deputized you. Thought you be at least five-nine by now."

Tommy was not tall, but for reasons known to none, he often joked about his height in a self-depreciating way. He told his new friends he wasn't tall enough to be taken seriously. He had an infectious smile when it suited him.

"Good afternoon to you too, Addis. You seem taller to me. You might want to bend your knees a little so I can hear you tell me why 'n hell I had to ride the train down here from God's country and take a buggy ride from the depot in an open coach driven by a consumptive feller on his last legs."

"Well, Mr. George, we have a ruckus down here, and it involves a man I'm sure you know. Tom Horn. He's the talk of newspapermen and lawmen in both my state in yours. Any reason you cannot take on an assignment lookin' into the famous range detective?"

"Depends," Tommy said, shaking his head slowly from side to side. "The *Laramie Boomerang* and the *Cheyenne Daily Leader* have been selling newspapers by the bucket load with all the whooping and carrying on over the murder of Kels Nickell's boy. Horn's sitting in jail in Cheyenne waiting for trial."

"You got an opinion on him, Tommy? Did he do the deed or was he framed?"

"Most everyone in Wyoming has an opinion on the subject. Me? I dunno. Making a judgment based on newspaper gossip is like trusting a dime novel to tell you the truth."

"Sound judgment, Tommy. We have need of you. To tell you the truth, we were hoping you hadn't picked a side in the case. Let me tell you why we cannot ride up there to your fine grassland and snoop around ourselves."

"Hell, I already know why you can't do that. Jurisdiction, right? We have it and you don't."

"Well, yes that's right, but when it comes to Tom Horn, he's broken the law, made the law, and been on both sides of it in both my state and yours. And he's got powerful big cattle ranchers on his side in both states. Here's the nub of it. Our investigations down here are at a standstill now that Mr. Horn's sitting in jail waiting for trial on the Willie Nickell case. We have at least one murder case we know he did that's coming up for indictment by a grand jury here in Denver. But we don't want to do anything to mess up or irritate our fellow prosecutors in Cheyenne. So that's where you come in. We need someone who knows the ground in Laramie County to keep watch on things for us. And there's one other thing. We got a call from the U.S. Attorney here in Denver alerting us, on the quiet, that they're considering sending a man up to the Iron Mountain area to scout something out they're interested in. We're not sure what, but it involves Tom Horn from a different angle."

Tommy stood up, took off his canvas travel jacket, and fished a small black cigar out of his vest pocket. Lighting it with a stick match, he took in a long draw and asked Addis, "Okay if I smoke this cigar?"

"It's gonna stink up the room, but if it soothes you and puts you in a yes-sir kind of mood, it's alright with me. What do you think about going back to work for us while this Tom Horn business sorts itself out?"

"Addis, let me tell you something you'd have no reason to know. I can't say I know Tom Horn, but I've been within

30.30 range of him several times. I know he's never lined me out, because I'm sitting here in your office today. He's a fine shot, sits a saddle straight up, and makes everyone around him either scared or sweet on him. He came to our part of Wyoming to threaten sheepherders, kill cattle rustlers, and continue the dominance of big cattle ranchers. I'm sure you know all this already, but here's something you might not know. Horn's reputation alone can persuade a man looking to steal a few cattle to head south for the Colorado border. Once I saw him riding down a long draw, maybe four miles to a little lake I was headed to just to catch a few fish. It was three miles from my little ranch north of Bosler. I was a quarter mile away on the top of the ridge to his right. I knew it was him by the way he sat his horse, a big black, with a roach mane. He was just walking along enjoying the morning sun. Across the other side of the ridge, I saw two men dismount and ground tie their horses. One of 'em had a spy-glass and turned it in Horn's direction. They watched him ride on by. Once he was a mile or so down the draw, they jumped their horses and spurred them the other direction. Those boys were dissuaded of stealing a cow anywhere in the same county, just by getting a look at Tom Horn."

"I'm sure you're right, Tommy. Do you know about the killings at Brown's Hole in the summer of 1900? It's pretty close to the border, but I've never been there myself."

"Yes, but I don't know the particulars."

Addis, picking up his thick porcelain coffee cup, took what must have the last swallow of cold coffee and rolled a cigarette. Flicking a wooden match with his thumbnail, he lit up and took a long draw. Pursing his lips, he blew the gray smoke out like a teakettle just boiling.

"Their names were Matt Rash and Isam Dart. They'd been up there, just shy of the Wyoming border, for three, maybe four years. Our office and the county sheriff up there had no cause to arrest them, but we knew they were running with one or two other ragged ne'er-do-wells at Brown's Hole. At the time, the range war in Colorado and across the border in Wyoming was getting folks riled up. It looked like it could turn unfriendly. Maybe even another Johnson County War that your Wyoming cowmen had earlier on the west side of your fine state. But the country around Brown's Hole is different. In Wyoming, the big ranches were using stock detectives to drive out homesteaders from settling on lands they thought they owned, or at least had the sole right to the grass close to their fee-deeded ranches. But here in Colorado, in places like Brown's Hole, we'd had a good many small ranches for many years."

"Addis, you're a fine storyteller and all, but is there something you want from me about Brown's Hole?"

"Well, just you hold on, Tommy. I'm getting there. What happened was, big outfits trying to expand on both sides of the border discovered a big open range around Brown's Hole. The locals called the area Brown's Park, but the bigger ranches looking to move in called it Brown's Hole because the two or three small shacks there became a safe haven for rustlers. Rash and Dart were among 'em."

"So, Addis, you're saying those men, Rash and Dart, were habitual cattle rustlers."

"Don't know you can call 'em habitual anything, but that was their reputation. The start of the killings at Brown's Hole was here in Denver because Tom Horn was here. Three or four big ranch cattlemen with stock and range on both sides of the border made a decision that brought Tom Horn into the mix. One of the men was a man I'm sure you know, name of John C. Coble. He was a partner, I think, of Frank Bosler in the Iron Mountain country you call home."

"Know him well. My ranch is a damn sight smaller, but we share a property line, and we push one another's cows back and forth once in a while. I think he's a man of his word, but he's against anyone who steals cows, or runs sheep. That's his root, for sure."

Addis stubbed out his cigarette between his thumb and the shank of his first finger. "I thought you'd know him. But I'm guessing you don' know that he put Tom Horn on his payroll, provided him horses, a cot in his bunkhouse, a place at the kitchen table, and other necessities. Like ammunition and cover."

"Cover? What kind of cover," Tommy asked.

"Cover as a range detective. Some called him a stock detective. The name doesn't matter. John Coble and his Wyoming association paid Tom Horn's costs and covered for him when he killed rustlers, or run off sheep, sheepherders, and sheep owners. Our investigation into the killings of Rash and Dart explained what the association that Coble led wanted out of Horn. They told him that Brown's Hole was a nest of lawlessness, and he had their backing to clean 'em out, no questions asked. We can't prove it with witness testimony, but we know Coble told Horn he'd get five hundred dollars for every known cattle thief he killed. Brown's Hole was a good place to start."

Tommy gave Addis a headshake and a narrow eye.

"You're saying flat out, the attorney general's office knows Tom Horn's a hired killer, paid and directed by John Coble?"

"I'm saying our investigation turned up what could be called circumstantial evidence that Coble and a half-dozen other ranchers in the area knew about Tom Horn's activities in that area and ponied up the money to pay him to rid the area of rustlers. Can't say they knew anything about the particular killing of Rash or Dent."

"Well, what *do* you know about Horn and the killings of those two men?"

"We know Tom Horn used an alias—James Hicks. We know he posed at Brown's Hole as a horse buyer. Made it known he was a good hand, too. A man that drove a supply wagon from Rock Springs to Brown's Hole gave us that information. He described Horn as quiet. Not happy. And he was sure it was Horn that shot Dart. You ever heard of Dart? Did he do any work in your part of the country?"

Addis looked at Tommy with a squint.

"Am I supposed to know him?"

"I'm just asking, Tommy, because there ain't many men like him. Dart was a Negro cowpuncher. How he partnered up with Rash, a white man from Texas, nobody knows. Best we can tell, it started out with Rash and Dart arguing with one another over some cows they'd sold in Brown's Hole in the spring of 1900. One said the other cheated on the split. While that wrangling was going on, Horn learned that someone from Brown's Hole was stealing cattle with the VD brand on 'em."

"VD's John Coble's brand. One of 'em, anyhow," Tommy said.

"Yeah, we checked the registration in Cheyenne. Our notion of it is that the investigation Horn was doing for Coble led him to Rash and Dart. People up there said Horn was the shooter, when the local sheriff investigated. We pitched in on that. But nobody was willing to testify in court 'bout the rustling. Then came the first killing. Matt Rash was at his little cabin at Cold Spring Mountain. On July 8, 1900, someone shot him there, sitting on his porch eating lunch. The body showed the first bullet hit him under the arm and the second in the back. Whoever did it also killed Rash's horse."

"You're sure it was Horn who done the deed?"

Addis stood up and grabbed hold of his head, wringing his neck from one side to the other, and gritting his teeth. He mumbled something about the Goddamned artheritis before answering Tommy's question.

"Pretty sure. We're taking it to a grand jury in the next few months."

"What about Dart? How'd you tie Horn to that?"

"Well, Dart was a local character, for sure. He was the elected constable in Sweetwater County, Wyoming. And he was charged with illegally branding cows there, but the charges were dropped. That was in 1899. The next year, Tom Horn swore out a complaint against Dart for horse theft. Then, on October 4th, someone found Dart holed up with six other men in a cabin near Brown's Hole. Dart died of a single rifle shot wound, when he walked out of the cabin in a line with the other men. It was cold and the wind was hard. They all scattered. No one knew where the shot came from. Next day, a deputy found two .30 caliber shells at the base of a tree not far from the cabin."

"And you knew Horn packed a 30.30, so you figured it was him? Was it that simple?"

"No, but we know Horn was in the area. We know he shot Rash. Dart was part of the gang that Rash was also a part of at Brown's Hole. Someone saw a lone horseman in the area. It might be enough to get a probable cause ruling by a grand jury."

"OK, maybe you can clear something else up for me. There's been talk about the Hole-in-the-Wall gang up in Wyoming. Is that the same gang as the Brown's Hole gang, or is it the same place, just with a different name?"

"No, it's not the same. The Hole-in-the-Wall gang was up in Northern Wyoming, in Johnson County, some years back."

"So, Tom Horn got arrested two years later, on January 18, 1902. What happened to the Brown's Hole killings in that two years? If Horn was your best suspect, why the two-year wait to ferret things out?"

"Well, Tommy," Addis said, "we probably will indict Horn now, just in case a jury in Wyoming lets him off. Who knows? Thing is, we need you to keep your eyes open for evidence that might come up in the trial you got coming up in Cheyenne— the Willie Nickell murder. Could be they will develop some evidence that could connect Horn to the killings down here. And there are other investigations going on now that Horn's been jailed. People might feel safer now. People who know things might be willing to talk to us and your own lawmen in Laramie County."

"Could be. But I'm a Wyoming rancher. Only work I did for your office involved local rustlers, crooks, train robbers, and scalawags here in Colorado. And the case your office is working on here does not involve Wyoming people, does it?"

"It might. See, Tom Horn did range detective work here too. And there are ranches in Wyoming that cross the border into Colorado. I suspect that we'll eventually find out Tom Horn killed or run off more 'n what we know about now. Since he's in jail, could be some tongues will wag. If so, we think we need a Wyoming man to let us know if anyone wags in our direction. We know the deputy U.S. marshal, man named George Ramsey, here in Denver is willing to work with us. They have a man headed up your way. His name's Angus something. Didn't get the last name."

"Neither did I. But I met him yesterday at the Brown Palace. Seems a fair hand and intends to do some investigative work in Cheyenne into Tom Horn's confession."

"Yes, we know about that," Addis said. "We think the two of you ought to talk to one another, since both of you will be following the Tom Horn case. Do you know when the trial will be?"

"No, I don't. Doubt it'll be soon. Case like that takes time. And Tom Horn's got the best defense lawyers in Wyoming, courtesy of John Coble. How long you thinking of paying me a daily wage to listen and watch up in Cheyenne? You know I got a horse ranch to run in Bosler. It's a half day ride to Cheyenne."

"Could be weeks, maybe a month. Depends on the trial, and whatever you can find up there that might loop up to what we're dallying down here. Make your reports in writing, and send telegrams when you need to."

CHAPTER 5

ANGUS GOT OFF THE Union Pacific passenger car at the train depot in Cheyenne an hour after sundown. He walked two blocks up to the Register Hotel on West 16th Street and asked for a room.

"Sorry, Mister, but all we got left is the communal room. Twelve bunks, two toilets, two showers, and a footlocker for your tack. We ask you to leave your guns here at the desk. It's two-fifty a night."

"Well, that'll do me just fine. How come you're all filled up? Something going on in town?"

"Mister, you got the look of a cowboy to me, but maybe you ain't from around here or you'd know this is rodeo week. The Cheyenne Frontier Days—biggest rodeo in the Rockies. The saloons are busting open, and every hotel is near full. The communal room is empty right now, seeing as how it's dinner and drinking time for both the cowboys and the fans. There will be a lot of what we do best in Cheyenne tonight—drinkin', dancin', fightin', and lying about how many bulls or broncs you rode last year."

"All right, sounds entertaining. Is that why you're taking guns here at the hotel—gun fights?"

"No, you can take your gun to dinner, or the saloon. But not to the communal room. There's lots of law in town—extra deputies. Some places ask you to leave your belly gun behind, and they don't like anyone carrying a rifle anywhere. You know, don't you, we got a famous assassin here in the Cheyenne city jail? Name of Tom Horn. They say he killed a boy in cold blood and put a rock under his head to prove he did it. You heard about it, right? Hell, everybody here knows he did it. They'll be picking a jury soon. Maybe they'll pick me to be on it. I'll give him the noose in under eight seconds."

"Got your mind made up on it, do you? I'm curious. What made him do it?"

"Don't know the details, but everyone says he's a hired killer. Who else would shoot an unarmed boy down from ambush?"

Angus paid his two-fifty and took his bag and the rolled-up tarp with his 30.40 in it to the communal room. He would not give his gun to a hotel clerk who talked too much. If anybody complained, he always had the Deputy United States Marshal badge in his vest pocket. He had a light dinner—roasted game hen, mashed potatoes with lots of pepper, corn bread, and buttermilk to wash it down. Then he walked to the Double Arrow Saloon three doors down and decided the hotel clerk was right. It was full of men half-drunk, loud, with two poker games at tables in the back. A two-man band—guitar and fiddle—played what passed for dancing music. None of the couples looked like they knew one another. The men were cowpunchers. The women were what in New Mexico they called "ladies of the night." From time to time one couple or another would peel off and take the stairway up to the second floor.

Angus nursed his beer mug standing at the bar and reading the *Wyoming Tribune*. A hand slapped him on the back.

"Angus, figured you'd be in one saloon or another on this fine rodeo night. I got a telegram yesterday that you'd be in town today. I rode a fine little roan horse down here. You come in on the Union Pacific?"

"Ah, Tommy George. Good to see you. Now I know one man in a town plumb full of strangers tonight. You're right about me coming in on the train. It's a long, slow pull up here from Denver, and it's loud. Not at all like riding a long-stepping pony across some of the most beautiful meadows I've ever seen. I hope they got a livery stable where I can rent a horse while I'm here."

"No need. I ponied a big bay from my ranch in Bosler for you. I named him Tucson. That's a town in Arizona where Tom Horn spent some time. He's yours for however long you decide to stay in Cheyenne. Got any guess how long that'll be?"

"No, I've never been any good at guessing. You got any sense of how long you'll be in town doing your part of this look-see-what-we-can-find kind of job?"

"Well, things are slow at my barn—I raise and sell well-broke horses for a dozen ranches in the Iron Mountain area. I have a good man tending the herd. I'll spend two or three days here and then go back to the ranch for a few days. Back and forth suits me just fine. Thought you might like to ride up there with me. I'll show you where the boy was shot and introduce you to some people who know the territory."

"Damn, Tommy," Angus said. "You just made my day. I can't wait to get horseback. I get a little jittery when I spend too much time in a town this size. And this rodeo crowd is having too much fun for me. How about we meet for breakfast in the morning? You free?"

"I am. Say about 7 am at the Plains Hotel. It's two blocks west of this place."

"Sounds might fine, Tommy. See you there."

CHAPTER 6

A NGUS SPENT A RESTLESS night in the communal room at
The Register. After midnight the rodeo crowd stumbled in,
laughing, singing, and cussing. Some fell onto the bunks, others jammed into the two-toilet room, making loud noises and
emitting foul smells. Boots dropping, arguments over chosen
bunks, and the clatter of windows being opened by some and
shut by others added to the din. Nobody paid any attention to
him. He woke up in the half-light an hour before dawn. Now
he heard the snoring, belching, farting, and banging around
that defines a bunkhouse full of men with hangovers and full
bladders. He dressed quietly and quickly, packed his gear and
his .30.40 into the tarp roll, and left the hotel. Knowing the
cafes would be still closed, he headed for the only place he
was sure would have a coffee pot at the boil this early in the
day—the livery stable two blocks down.

The stable keeper, a tight brisk little man, was just pour-
ing himself a cup of cowboy coffee when Angus opened the
stable door.

"Mornin,'" Angus said.

"Ain't it, though. You must not be a rodeo cowboy," the man said, "those boys are all sleeping off hangovers and wondering if they can stick for eight seconds with a head that feels all caved in. Five or six of 'em are right here sleeping in the stalls with their rope horses."

"No, my rodeo days are long past, I'm just looking for a cup of pre-dawn coffee and to get a look at a horse I'm going to be using for a while. A friend named Tommy George owns the horse. I think he might have stabled it here."

"Sure, friend. I've known Tommy George for maybe ten years. He's a fine example of sitting a horse and a damn fine judge of 'em too. He came in yesterday riding a sweet little roan mare and ponying a big bay. She's out back in the mare corral. Only roan out there right now. Coffee's strong enough to stand on its own. Sugar's in the brown box there. Help yourself."

Angus spent the next two hours drinking the bitter coffee, with three sugar lumps, and brushing the bay Tommy called Tucson. Then he brushed the little roan. He brushed all the mares and delivered their morning feed—a small sack of grain and a pitch-fork full of alfalfa hay. At seven-thirty he walked back up to the street to a half-full café called Lee's Café & Breads. Apparently it served meals and sold sliced bread. It smelled more like a bakery than a restaurant. A spindly man with a curved back, wearing a shop apron, got up from the front table just as Angus walked in.

"This table is free, Mister," he said. "And you can have the paper too. Just leave it here for the next man to read. I got to get back to the ovens before Lee starts hollering at me. He's a fine cook, but he sure likes to holler at the help."

Angus sat and ordered three flattened eggs, biscuits, and milk before turning to the newspaper. The headline did its job and got Angus's full attention. SENSATIONAL PLOT TO DELIVER TOM HORN FROM COUNTY JAIL. The smaller print subtitle below that declared, ONE OF THE BOLDEST AND MOST DARING SCHEMES EVER CONCOCTED IN CRIMINAL HISTORY. A TRUE BUT ALMOST INCREDULOUS STORY.

The *Wyoming Tribune*, Cheyenne's largest daily paper, laid out the story in three pages, with pictures, which left only one page for the rest of the news in Wyoming's capital city. Angus read the first page and most of the second before he realized the paper was two weeks old. The story identified a man named Herr as the leader of the effort. He'd been arrested for stealing a saddle, confessed to the crime, and got sixty days in the county jail. Apparently, on purpose. They said Herr was just "a tool through which Tom Horn's plotters expected to communicate with Mr. Horn how they planned to deliver him from imprisonment."

The paper implied the plotters were from Bosler, Tommy George's home territory. Apparently the man named Herr got out short of his sixty-day sentence and took written details back to Horn's deliverers—instructions written on toilet paper and the backside of a letter. The paper claimed that Herr got scared of going back to jail if he helped deliver Mr. Horn, so "overcome with fear of punishment, Mr. Herr voluntarily revealed the details of the dark plot" to the paper and then slipped away from Cheyenne. It didn't say whether the men in Bosler ever got the letter or the toilet paper. The instructions rambled on about sticks of dynamite, blowing the east wall, and tying up a saddled horse close by for Horn to "ride off into the night." He'd head to Bosler, the newspaper said, with help located under "a snowball and a stepping stone."

Angus finished his breakfast, left a dollar fifty on the table, next to the newspaper, and walked back down to the livery stable. Tommy George was there, exercising the big bay on a thirty-foot rope in the corral next to where the mares were kept.

"Good to see you're up, Angus. Lefty told me you'd come in before dawn looking for quiet and coffee and that you'd given both my horses a good brushing. Much appreciated. Got any plans for the morning?"

"No particular ones. Thought I'd get the lay of the town, and maybe listen to whatever gossip there is about the Tom Horn case. But I'm open to your ideas."

"Well, I don't like to leave my horses in a mixed stable with horses they don't know for too long. Maybe we could take a half-day ride to keep the horses happy?

"Mighty fine idea, Tommy. Let's saddle up whenever you're ready."

Cheyenne was surrounded by one of the greenest and windiest prairies Angus had ever seen. The horizon stretched for miles, the hills were rolling, and the grass belly-high to Tommy's big bay gelding. Flocks of birds moved fluidly across a blue sky dotted with clouds billowing up like towers. Angus, no stranger to grassy meadows, felt a little intimidated. This was a vast expanse of soft, undulating grassland. He could make out countless herds of cattle. Two bunches of antelopes grazed along with a few horses, intermingling as though this world belonged to them, not us.

"Tommy, I read the morning newspaper, the *Wyoming Tribune*, but it turned out to be two weeks old. The whole damn thing was about a planned delivery of Tom Horn, and it said the planners were Bosler people. Was it a true plan that failed, or a yarn spun to sell newspapers?"

"Read it today, did you? Can't say I read it. But I'd say it was true *and* a plan to sell newspapers. There's been lots of that going around from the day they arrested him. That's not the first time folks have taken the law into their own hands in Wyoming."

"The part of the story that got my attention was *delivery*. That means taking a man out of jail by force to lynch him. But the story also implies they might have been planning an *escape*, rather than a delivery."

"I suspect it was an escape. But either way it's law breaking. As for Bosler people, there's a mix there. I know people on both sides. The boy's family and kin want Horn strung up. Horn's employers don't want it known they paid him to kill innocent boys. So they'd like to see all this over with. Not sure they'd break him out, though. So maybe it was a delivery."

"We don't see that much these days down in New Mexico."

"Reckon so. No range war down there, right?"

"Our ranchers are mostly accepting sheep. Our grass is not at all like yours. And our herds ain't giant either. Mexican sheepherders have been with us a long time. And Mexican cowboys have their own ranches. Some raise both sheep and cattle on the same spread."

"Well, Wyoming ain't that gentle. It's one or the other up here. And we have a history still in the making. Last May, a young sheep man over in the Big Horse Basin was grazing his brother's herd on a meadow claimed by cattlemen. That's a cattle offense far as big ranchers are concerned. He was killed, they say, by a man named McCloud. I never heard of him—he wasn't a range detective like Tom Horn. Anyhow, McCloud got himself arrested for the murder and they hauled him down here to Cheyenne to await trial. Not long after the sheep man killing there was another killing in Weston County. Thirty-five cowboys hit the Weston County jail and took that prisoner to a railroad bridge, noosed him up, and threw him off the bridge. The fall decapitated him. A month or so later, a lynch mob hit the Big Horn County jail in Basin. They shot up the jail and killed a deputy sheriff. There's a lot of grousing about courts not getting justice quick enough to hired killers, like Tom Horn."

"You saying Wyoming jails are easy to crack from the outside?"

"Can't say that exactly. But sheriffs and deputies are at risk when they got a man waiting for trial in a court system that's a might slow. The people want swift and severe punishment for killing children. The jails in most counties are small and not fit for keeping killers locked up for a long time. That's why many of them get moved down here to Cheyenne. It has more experienced men on guard and more places to get the makins for smoking and grub to eat. Which, I should add, the sheriff has to pay for out of his government budget."

They found a small creek where they rested the horses and ate jerky and hard tack. Then they rode back to town and Angus moved out of The Register and into the Plains Hotel that afternoon. He spent the afternoon in the Capitol Library reading up on Wyoming history. Tommy said they ought to meet next morning for breakfast at Lee's Café and Breads.

"I'll bring a copy of tomorrow's newspaper so we'll both know what's happening."

As it turned out, Tommy got there first, ordered coffee, and was reading the menu when Angus walked in the front door. That's when they heard the first gunshots. Close by. They became eye witnesses to what would become the big story the next day.

Shortly after eight that warm August morning, Horn and Jim McCloud escaped jail. Nobody knew that Tom Horn and Jim McCloud, both accused of killing young boys, had been paired in two cells on the top floor of the Cheyenne jail. They were by themselves up there. The only way to reach their cells was up a rickety flight of stairs and then through a tight hallway. A new mechanical device controlled both doors at once. There was a small sitting hall where they could sit down and talk, but they had to stay in their cells to eat and sleep. McCloud was taking daily medicine for something, Tommy said.

Seems everyone in the café that morning was reading about the escape, or explaining it to the next table over. The jailer on duty that morning, R. A. Proctor, opened both doors and stepped into the small room in front of the cells. They jumped him. Horn nearly killed him with a chokehold before tying his arms behind his back with a window-shade cord. They drug him back down the stairway and into the sheriff's office. A 30.40 Winchester, loaded with five shells, was on a rack. Procter's own gun, a Belgian automatic pistol, was locked inside a small safe. They wanted more shells for the .30.40. Procter told them all the ammo was in the safe. They forced him to open it. He did and grabbed his pistol and turned it back toward them. The two prisoners struggled with Proctor for the pistol. He got off two shots during the struggle and one grazed McCloud. Another deputy, Leslie Snow, ran into the office and into McCloud, who was now armed with the .30.40 rifle. But before he could shoot, Snow turned back out and slammed the door shut. McCloud turned, went back into the jail, and ran off with the .30.40.

Horn, still wrestling with Procter in the office, got the pistol, but Procter somehow engaged the safety on the automatic pistol. Horn tried to shoot Procter but couldn't figure how to turn the safety off. So he hit Procter on the head, ran out the front door, and crossed Ferguson Street and down the adjacent alley.

A stable was close by, but when Horn ran into it he found McCloud had led the buckskin out the rear of the barn. Moments earlier, Laramie County Sheriff Johnny Smalley ran out of his house behind the jail. He saw McCloud, drew his revolver, and fired.. The buckskin pitched and threw McCloud. Smalley ran into the office, secured a 30.30 from the rack, and ran back to where he'd last seen him.

That's when Tommy George and Angus arrived, running the short block from the café to the jail. Tommy was armed. Angus was not. Moments later, another deputy, Pat Hennessey, a mail clerk with a double-barreled shotgun, arrived. Horn was a block away. Someone shot at him. Hearing the shot, Tommy and Angus ran in that direction. Their first look at Horn was a surprise. He was frantically trying to turn the safety off the Belgian pistol. He was on Twentieth Street when they spotted him. They did not draw down on him, but a man across the street was closer. He fired one shot at Horn with a pocket pistol. His shot burrowed across Horn's head, and he dropped to the street, still trying to unlock the damned Belgian pistol. Both groups got to him about the same time. The two deputies jumped on top of Horn and pummeled him. Within two minutes a sizeable crowd arrived. Someone in the crowd screamed, "Rope!" Another hollered, "Hang the son of a bitch!" The deputies bound Horn tightly, and frog-walked him back to jail and up the stairs to his cell.

The next day, Angus decided he'd best expand his reading beyond the Cheyenne papers. In the *Denver Post*, he learned that Kels Nickell had been a block away when Horn was captured, and that he'd run to Sheriff Smalley's office to protest the lax way they'd been dealing with Horn. He made such a fuss that Sheriff Smalley threatened to arrest him and throw him in the same cell with Horn if he kept it up. Another deputy had fired at a man he thought was Horn but was actually T. F. Durbin, who'd heard the gunshots and was running away from the scene.

Rifles were passed out of a munitions locker to state militiamen when one prematurely discharged. Horn's quick capture was balanced against the revelations that there'd been other planned escapes the local press had missed. One reporter had it on good authority that a "fine bay horse, equipped with a cowboy saddle, had been tied to a rail near the jail, and was not taken away until after dark."

The papers went on about lynching, but Tommy George told Angus the whole damn thing firmed up people's thinking that Horn had to be hung legally. And by an odd coincidence, Horn and McCloud looked a lot alike. So much so, it was reported that the men who captured McCloud thought he was Horn until they drug him back to the jail.

Weeks later, a *Denver Post* reporter said he'd interviewed Horn in jail and Horn confirmed the dead-on accuracy of the *Post*'s reporting on his near escape. He insisted the reporter tell him where he got his information. The reporter said he'd also talked to R. A. Proctor, who "bore no grudge against Horn." Horn enjoyed that and responded, "Proctor could beat any two men I have ever seen. Tell him he won out and deserves all the credit he can get. It was a magnificent fight."

After four days in Cheyenne, Angus had no answers for Marshal Ramsey's questions. He'd made a written list. One, what happened up in Wyoming in the eighteen days between the coroner's inquest and Horn's confession? Two, why was a deputy U.S. marshal involved in a state murder case? Three, how did LeFors get Horn to confess? Four, how did a Laramie County deputy sheriff happen to be in the next room? Five, was it just good luck that a court stenographer was also next door simultaneously?

The first question turned out to be easy. Wyoming was a small state. About 90,000 people lived there. LeFors had two jobs. He was a deputy U.S. marshal and also a deputy sheriff working for Sheriff Smalley. The court reporter, Charles Ohnhaus, worked in both courts—the U.S. federal court and the Laramie county court. The other witness that Angus got from Marshal Ramsey was a Laramie County deputy sheriff named Les Snow. Angus talked to LeFors first—otherwise they might be warned off by LeFors and not talk to him. The prosecutor was Walter Stoll. Angus had no intention of trying to talk to him; he was the appointed U.S. attorney for Wyoming in charge of all federal crimes. He was also the appointed county attorney for state crimes. Seems like everyone in Wyoming had more than one job.

CHAPTER 7

THE UNITED STATES MARSHALS office in Cheyenne was on the second floor of a three-story brick building called the Commercial Building on Sixteenth Street. It had a narrow jack-knife stairway up from street level but a wide three-bay window overlooking downtown Cheyenne. It housed many federal, state, and county offices. U.S. Marshal Frank A. Hadsell had appointed Joe LeFors as an office deputy in 1899, in part because he'd worked for other law enforcement agencies in Colorado and Wyoming. An "office deputy" wasn't expected to work full time. LeFors had other employment—most important an ongoing appointment by the chairman of the Laramie County Commission, Sam Corson. Corson hired LeFors specifically to investigate the Willie Nickell murder. He reported to both Walter Stoll, the county prosecutor, and Paul Bailey, the chief deputy to U.S. Marshal Hadsell. Angus's first meeting with LeFors had been arranged by wire and telephone between U.S. Marshal

George Ramsey in Colorado and his counterpart, Marshal Hadsell in Cheyenne.

Angus had a little information about LeFors. He was a Texan by birth and came to Wyoming in 1885 on a big cattle drive. His first work in Wyoming was punching cows on a sizeable ranch near Buffalo. In 1897, he'd been part of the posse that recovered a large herd of stolen stock from the Hole-in-the-Wall gang. Next, he hired on in Montana as a contract livestock inspector but mostly worked cows in northeast Wyoming. That's where he became friends with W. D. "Billy" Smith, a Montana brand inspector based in Miles City, Montana. Smith was LeFors's supervisor in Montana. That connection proved important in getting Tom Horn to "visit" with LeFors during the noon hour in his office on January 12, 1901, the day before they arrested Horn, and only eighteen days after Horn was cleared by the coroner's inquest.

Angus walked the three blocks from The Plains Hotel on Thirteenth Street to the U.S. Marshals office on Sixteenth Street. He walked up the narrow stairway to the office, told the lady in the black dress who he was, and who he wanted to see. She said Deputy LeFors was expecting him and that he'd be ready in a moment.

LeFors came through the second door down the hall to the small anteroom at the front. He was a tall man, dressed like a banker rather than a lawman. His brown hair was neatly tucked under a light tan hat with a two-inch flat brim. His close-set eyes were tucked above a thin nose that could barely support the large handle-bar mustache below it. It was a feature that said a lot about the man who had somehow extracted a confession from Tom Horn. It said he was smart and cared about how he looked. He wore a stiff-collared white shirt, neatly tied bow tie, and a waistcoat with a gold-fobbed watch chain threaded from the second button on the waistcoat to a watch pocket over his heart. His tailored wool suit hung on him like it'd been shaped just for him. His boots were polished and his grip was firm. Too dressed up for my taste, Angus thought, but he's got the serious cut of a man not to be trifled with.

"Angus, I'm Joe LeFors," he announced as he took long strides toward Angus. "I'm right pleased to meet you and hope to be of some service to your office in Denver. Come on back to my office, I want you to meet my boss."

Angus followed LeFors into the office. When they came in, a portly man with a florid face rose from one of the two chairs before the small desk. As LeFors walked around to the business side of the desk, he said, "This is my boss, Chief Deputy United States Marshal Bailey. Ya'll don't mind him sitting in on our little confab, do you?"

"No. Nice to meet you, Deputy Bailey. I appreciate your time. I'm told by my boss, George Ramsey, that you know why I'm up here, right?"

Bailey answered, "Well, I've known George Ramsey for twenty odd years. He sent me a wire, then we talked on the phone line a little. He just asked for our cooperation regarding the confession my deputy here took from the defendant Tom Horn. He didn't say why, but he didn't need to. Mind if I ask *you* why you're here?"

"Not at all. I'm here because Tom Horn has potential criminal charges in Colorado. He will most likely get indicted by a federal grand jury soon. But they won't ask for extradition down there for trial until his case up here is decided. My boss and the attorney general for Colorado are both interested because what happens here might influence what ought to happen down there."

LeFors, seated behind his desk, leaned forward. "Angus, are you a sworn deputy, a stock detective, or what? Mind telling us your official status in the Horn case?"

Angus fished into his vest pocket, pulled out his badge, and slid it across the desk to LeFors.

"I'm a sworn deputy, but my boss suggested I not wear the badge around town up here. We didn't think a shiny badge on my vest would help get information up here. See, my badge is identical to yours. It says Deputy U.S. Marshal, but there's no location stated. If I wore it up here, folks might mistake me for you."

LeFors laughed easy. "Aw hell, that'd never happen. You have no mustache, and bigger ears than me. I'm known for how I look—my wife says my mustache is bigger that my ears."

Angus smiled. "I guess a man can grow a fine handle-bar mustache, but he's stuck with whatever ears God gave him."

"All right then," LeFors said. "There's a little piece of business we outta settle first off. We've cleared this with Walter Stoll, the prosecutor. He says we can answer your questions with the understanding that it stays within law enforcement in our state, and yours. We ain't giving interviews to the defense lawyers hired to defend Tom Horn. They had me on cross-examination at Horn's preliminary hearing for nearly two full days. I've got a copy of the transcript of Horn's confession right here on my desk. I might use it to answer your questions, but you can't have our copy. Expect you can get one from the court clerk, right?"

"Yes, we can. But what we're interested in might not be in the transcript. No matter. I can assure you I'm not talking to the defense lawyers in the Wyoming case. Only men I report to are in the U.S. Marshals office in Denver."

"Fine," Bailey answered.

LeFors nodded. "Where would you like me to start?"

"Well, I suppose it's with the big question. How 'n hell did you get Horn to talk to you? If he did the deed, he's a fool to talk about it with a deputy U.S. marshal. If he didn't, he's still a fool to talk to you about anything. He must have known you would tell your boss what he said, right?"

"Angus," LeFors said, as he reached down into his desk drawer, "Horn's no fool, but he had a narrow focus on getting a new job. Win or lose on this case, his days as a stock detective for John Coble are done. He talked to me because he thought I'd get him a job in Montana findin' and shootin' cattle thieves."

"Did that come out at the preliminary hearing?"

"At the end of my testimony, the prosecutor produced the letters about the Montana job. I talked a little about the letters, but not much. Then they turned me over to Horn's defense lawyer, a man named John Lacey. He grilled me about the confession, but not about how the confession came to be. You're the first one to ask about that. You want me to just lay it out for you?"

"That'd be mighty fine."

It took nearly an hour, but the story behind the conversation was more interesting than the confession itself. Turns out that LeFors had talked with Tom Horn twice before the one in this office everyone was calling the confession. They talked about the boy's shooting at different saloons in Cheyenne, but those conversations didn't yield much for the prosecution. LeFors got the idea to entice Horn to come to them. He had a friend from his days as a stock detective in Montana named W. D. Smith. He explained the situation to Smith, and asked him to write a letter about a made-up job in Montana. It was not a real job, just something to make Horn want to talk with LeFors on a friendly basis. The letter, dated December 28, 1901, to LeFors from Smith said,

> Friend Joe,
>
> I want a good man to do some secret work. And I want a man I can trust. And he must be a man not known in this country. The nature of this is, there is a gang over on the Big Moon River stealing cattle and we purpose to fit the man out as a wolfer and let him go into that country. If he is the right man he can soon get in with the gang. He must be a man that can take care of himself in any kind of country. The pay will be $125 per month. Joe, if you know of anyone who will fill the place let me know. There will be several months' work.
>
> Yours truly,
> W. D. Smith

Angus read the letter slowly. "But this letter is to you. How'd Horn know about it?"

"I gave the letter to John Coble at his Iron Mountain Ranch when I was up in Bosler investigating the case. I put it in a sealed envelope and asked him to give it to Horn. He did. Next thing I know, Horn wrote me a letter in his own hand, dated four days later, on New Years' day."

Iron Mountain Ranch Company
Bosler, Wyoming
Jan. 1st 1902
Joe LeFors, Esq.
Cheyenne, Wyoming
Dear Joe

Rec'd yours from W.D. Smith Miles City Mont. by Johnny Coble today. I would like to take up that work and I feel sure I can give Mr. Smith much satisfaction. I don't care how big or bad his men are or how many of them there are. I can handle them. They can scarcely be any worse than the Brown's Hole Gang and I stopped cow stealing there in one summer. If Mr. Smith cares to give me the work, I would like to meet them as soon as commencement so as to get into the country and get located before Summer. The wages of $125 per month will be all satisfactory to me. Put me in communication with Mr. Smith whom I know well by reputation and I can guarantee him the recommendation of every cow man in the State of Wyoming in this line of work. You may write Mr. Smith for me that I can handle his work and do it with less expense in the shape of lawyer and

witness fees than any man in the business. Joe,
you know yourself what my reputation is although
we have never been out together.
    Yours truly,
    Tom Horn

"Well," Angus said, "I can see how this would interest Mr. Horn. But didn't he know you were investigating the case for both the county and for Mr. Stoll, the prosecutor? Wasn't he a suspicious fellow?"

"Can't say much about his personality. But remember, the Coroner's inquest had called him to the stand and put him under oath. He testified for a long time there. But they didn't charge him. Once the inquest was closed, I expect he felt he was no longer a suspect. Since the prosecutor didn't have any hard evidence or eyewitness testimony, they didn't have much to support a charge. They wanted me to give the Montana job thing a try to see if I could get him talkin'. It worked."

"So, to put it another way, once the Coroner's inquest was closed, the prosecutor, Mr. Stoll, was not going to file charges against Horn?"

"Well, between us, I can say he felt damn sure Horn had shot the boy, but he didn't have enough hard evidence to get through a preliminary hearing. So we needed to find a way to get Horn talking. The man never knew when to shut up."

"And this confession. It's the only thing that changed in the eighteen days between the time they gave up on the inquest and the time they arrested Horn? Is that right?"

"Well, yes, but there's more letters, and one telegram. I figured once Horn saw it, he'd ride at full gallop down here from Bosler to get me to confirm the Montana job for him. And that's exactly what happened. See, W. D. Smith wrote to me on January the seventh confirming they wanted to hire Tom Horn and giving me direction to him on who to see, when to come, and other details. I got that conveyed to Tom Horn up at John Coble's ranch. Once he saw that, he wrote me. Here's his letter.

Iron Mountain Ranch Company
Bosler, Wyoming
January 7, 1902

Joe LeFors, Esq.
Cheyenne Wyo.

Friend Joe
    Rec'd yours Jan. 6th today and contents noted. Joe, I am much obliged to you for the trouble you have taken for me in this matter and I will do my best to give satisfaction. I will get the men for sure, for I have never yet let a cow thief get away from me unless he just got up and jumped clean out of the country. I will come to Cheyenne to get my pass as I can get one to Helena or any other from Cheyenne. I can go any time after ten days. I will see you in Cheyenne when I come in. Again thanking you for your trouble.
        I am yours truly,
        Tom Horn

"I got word that Tom Horn would come see me soon. Later, I learned that he rode from Bosler to Laramie on Jan 11, where he started hard drinking. They said he stayed up all night raising hell. Next day, he took the train down here to Cheyenne. Can't say where he stayed the night of the eleventh, but he was in the Tivoli Bar next morning. The bartender, name of Vincent McGwire, sent me a note from Horn saying he was there, so I sent word back. Could he come over to the Commercial Building on Sixteenth Street, and we'd talk?"

"So, you talked to him that morning, January 12. Was he sober?"

"Yes sir, he was. He'd been drinking some, but he can hold his liquor when he wants to, and he wanted to go up to Montana real bad. I'd say he was on his best behavior in my office. I'd arranged for two witnesses to listen in on our conversation."

"Without him—I mean, Tom Horn—knowing about it?" Angus asked.

"That's right. I knew we'd only get one chance at this and we had to get it just right. Tom Horn's a dangerous man, you know."

"Who were your witnesses?"

"Les Snow, a deputy sheriff here in Laramie County, and Charles Ohnhaus. Mr. Ohnhaus was the court stenographer. He took down every word we said on paper, and Les played close attention."

"Were they in the same room with you?"

"No, sir. No sir, they were not. There's an office next door to mine. I had Pete Bergson, a locksmith and a gunsmith, put a special lock on that door and shave some off the bottom of the door so Les and Mr. Ohnhaus could hear every word plainly.

They put some blankets on the floor to lay on and muffle any noise while I was talking to Tom Horn."

"Well, Joe, I want to hear what Mr. Horn told you, but if you don't mind, could you tell me why you were so sure Tom Horn was your man, that is, he's the one that shot that boy up on his father's ranch?"

"Sure, Angus. The killing was over the rangeland. Kels P. Nickell had turned to sheep. He had several thousand head up there next to his ranch, which was open government range. There was bad blood between cattlemen and sheepmen all over Wyoming, but mostly in the southeast, our part. To my mind the killing was about dollars and cents. And I was of a mind that the cattlemen up there wanted sheep out. Off the grazing land they thought they had first rights to. Now, I ain't of the opinion that all of them sanctioned all the ways being used. But they wanted the sheepmen out and the sheep gone. So my chief here at the U.S. Marshals office and Mr. Sam Corson of the Board of Commissioners for Laramie County told me to follow those leads in the boy's killing, and in the later attempted killing of his father."

"Well then," Angus said, "why don't you tell me how that conversation went, particularly the confession part?"

"Angus, it was a long conversation. I'll use our copy of the transcript to explain things to you. And I wrote my own notes after Tom Horn left my office. First off, he told me he'd gone barefoot to cover up his trail. He left his horse what he said was a 'Goddamned long ways off.' Horn kind of put things in a funny way, like he was remembering from some distance off. He said he supposed Willie Nickell was killed to keep him from making a commotion. The boy was shot about three hundred yards off. It was the best shot he ever made and the dirtiest trick he ever done. He used a .30-30. He got hungry, but never quit a job until he got his man."

"Hungry? Not sure what that means."

"Hell if I know. I took it to mean he didn't eat while he was out on a killing job."

"Did you ask him if he got paid to kill the boy?"

"Not plain out, but he did volunteer he got paid $2,100 for three dead men and another shot at five times. I asked him about the rock under Willie's head. He said it was done to collect the money for a job of this kind, and that he'd got paid before the job was done."

"You said Horn admitted going barefoot for some distance before he shot the Nickell boy. How'd that come up?"

"Well, I told him that I'd been up there to the Nickell ranch the day after they found the boy's body. I said I'd looked for tracks around the gate and around where they found the body. I told him that I'd tried to track him, and I never could find your trail—that's the way I put it. Told him I pride myself on being a tracker. That's when he said, 'No, Goddamn; I left no trail. The only way to cover up your trail is to go barefooted.' I said something about taking chances, and he corrected me right smart."

Angus got up, stretched his arms back behind him, and said maybe he would take a glass of water. LeFors walked over to the little cupboard next to his desk and poured one for him.

"OK, Angus, this is how I remember that part of the conversation went. Horn went back to his 'suppose' kind of talk. He said, I think it was this way. Suppose a man was in the big draw to the right of the gate—you know where it is—the draw that comes into the main creek below Nickell's house where Nickell was shot. Now suppose a man was in that, and the kid came riding up from this way, and suppose the kid started to run for the house, and the fellow headed him off at the gate, and killed him to keep him from going to the house, and raising a hell of a commotion. That's the way I think it happened."

"Deputy LeFors, I can see how if you were there listening to the man talk, you'd naturally assume he was talking about himself, but when he kept saying 'suppose this' and 'suppose that,' was it possible he was either bragging or covering up for someone else?"

"Angus, I knew for damn sure he was talking about himself the whole time. He is a talker about so much stuff that sometimes I think he was only talking to himself, not me—the man sitting right across from him. He'd look up at the tin ceiling here. He'd look out the bay window. But he was talking about himself. The defense lawyer at the preliminary hearing cross-examined me on this whole confession, and he tried to get me to back off because of those funny ways Horn talked, like supposing things happened the exact damn way they did happen."

"I don't mean to question you at all. I'm sure you reported it to the court just like you heard it. Does the transcript have all the supposing that went on?"

"You bet it does, Angus. And the judge heard it from me, from Deputy Les Snow, and from the testimony of Mr. Ohnhaus himself. He's a man that's used to being in a courtroom, and writing down everything said. That's what he did here, not more 'n ten feet from where you're sitting. He had excellent hearing and can write as fast as you can talk, only he writes in what they call shorthand."

"Did you ask him about the gun, the rifle he used?"

"I did. I asked him what kind of gun he had. He said 'a thirty-thirty Winchester.' I allowed as how a 30.40 might hold up better. He said he liked to get close to his man— 'the closer the better,' he said. 'How far was Willie Nickell killed?' I asked. 'About three hundred yards,' he answered. And I'm a thorough man, Angus. I asked about the shells and if he carried them away. 'You bet your Goddamn life I did,' he answered.

"Is that how your conversation ended?"

"No, I said, 'Tom, let's go downstairs and get a drink. I could always see your work clear, but I want you to tell me why you killed the kid. Was it a mistake?'"

At this, Angus leaned forward.

"Did you go and have a drink? And did he tell you whether it was a mistake?"

"I think he was tired of talking about it. This is the thing he said to me. 'Well, I will tell you all about it when I come back from Montana. It is too new yet.'"

"So you didn't go and have a drink?"

"We did. We went to Harry Hynds's saloon directly from my office. We had a drink, maybe two. Then we came back up here and Horn started talking about himself, almost like he wasn't in the room with me. Mr. Ohnhaus took that down too. Horn asked me what those sons of bitches were planning. 'Were they going to kill me? I am forty-four years, three months, and twenty-seven days old, and if I get killed now I have the satisfaction of knowing I have lived about fifteen ordinary lives. I would like to have had somebody who saw my past and could picture it to the public. It would be the most Goddamn interesting reading in the country. It'd be about the first man I killed when I was only twenty-six years old. He was a coarse son of a bitch.'"

"What did you say to that?"

"Well, I was hoping to get him talking again about killing Willie Nickell, or about shooting his dad a week later. I figured maybe a way to ease him back into that was to ask about money. I said, 'How much did you get for killing these fellows? In the Lewis and Powell case, you got six hundred dollars apiece.' But he didn't answer. He was getting tired out, I think. He'd been up most of the night, he'd told me earlier. So I answered my own question. I said, 'Tom, I have known everything you have done, for a great many years. I know where you were paid this money.'"

"What'd he say?"

"'Yes, I was paid this money on the train between Cheyenne and Denver.'"

"And that was for killings down in Colorado, right?"

"Suppose so."

"Joe, you're sounding a little like Tom Horn. Are you supposing, or did Tom Horn admit he was paid in Colorado for killings done there?"

"Right, we're lawmen and ought not to be supposing things. Sorry. The Lewis and Powell cases were done there. He was paid for them on the train between here and Denver. Most of that train ride is on the Colorado side. That's all I've got to say about it."

"Fine, Joe, you've been generous with your time. I'll report that to my boss in Denver."

"All right, Angus. You're welcome to come back here anytime."

"Oh, wait, Joe, there is one thing more. This conversation took place on a Sunday, right? When did the court stenographer type up his notes for the court?"

"Oh, we were in a hell of a hurry. Ohnhaus did it right away. That night. You see, Horn was planning on taking the afternoon train to Montana the next day. He was staying at the Inter Ocean Hotel at the corner of Capitol Avenue and Sixteenth Street. Ed Smalley and his deputy arrested Horn the next morning at the hotel. They'd been watching the stairs from dawn."

"Did Sheriff Smalley say how Horn reacted?"

"He did. After he locked the door on Horn's cell a few minutes later, Horn said he 'smelled a rat all right. It was Joe LeFors wasn't it? It was a set up.'"

"Well," Angus said, "he was right about that part, wasn't he? It was good detective work. A good set up, I'd say."

CHAPTER 8

A NGUS TOOK A HALF DAY to write a report to Marshal Ramsey in Denver about how Joe LeFors extracted a confession out of Tom Horn. He posted it himself at the railway depot and took the opportunity to send a telegram to Tommy George at the Bosler station. Tommy had mentioned that everyone in Bosler knows everyone else. It's a bunch of large and small ranches inside a thirty-mile swatch of fee ground and open range. Two hours after Angus wired Tommy, he got a knock on his door from the boy sent up by the front desk. He said a Mr. George is on the phone in the lobby if you care to take it.

"Tommy," Angus said, "glad you got my wire, and a little surprised that you could call back so soon. I think Wyoming has more phone lines than my home country in New Mexico. I had a long talk with Deputy LeFors and another man about Tom Horn's confession. I want to tell you all about it, but don't think we can do it over the phone. Maybe I could take the train up to Laramie and meet you there. I'd sure like your take on it."

"I'd be happy to hear how 'n hell the U.S. Marshals office got Tom Horn to sit down for an interview."

"That part's easy. They tricked him into it. What's not so easy is whether it's really him talking, or them."

"Tell you what, Angus, I could meet you in Laramie tomorrow afternoon. You catch the train up. Check into the Kilmer Hotel. I'll meet you there for dinner tomorrow night. Good people own the place—lifelong friends of mine. And I have an idea. How about we spend a few days in the saddle? There's some country here I'd like to show you. It'll help you imagine what happened. The Nickell and Miller ranches are close by my place near Bosler. And there's other places concerning Mr. Tom Horn that you ought to see. Sound good to you?"

"Good? There's nothing I'd rather do than get out of this hotel and swing a leg over a cow horse."

"All right then. You know the University of Wyoming is there in Laramie. They have a good library. Expect they might have some useful information regarding the ranching business. It's fair to say the big ranches mostly send their kids there and hope they'll come back home with a degree in how to run a ranch, large, or small wantin' to grow."

Tommy wasted no time at Kilmer Hotel's dining room the next evening. He and Tommy sorted out their common assignments on Tom Horn.

"Angus, I'd like to introduce you to some men here in Laramie that might be willing to talk to you about this whole business. One of 'em is a man named George Prentiss. I've known him for several years when he was a cow boss working for John Coble. You know Horn worked for Coble and mostly rode his stock; he bunked there and took most of his meals at Coble's ranch. Prentiss is now an employee of the Swan Livestock Company, a little bit north of here. I talked to him a week ago and he told me that he'd shared a seat on the train out of Bosler Station with Joe LeFors last November. LeFors was asking questions about Tom Horn. Prentiss told me LeFors said there were several Pinkertons interested in Horn down in Cheyenne. He said a Pinkerton had told him that Horn was drinking heavy and talking about the Nickell family. Something about the boy, Willie, but also about the father, Kels, and his troubles over those damn sheep he was keeping. The details weren't all that clear but Prentiss's view on the matter was. He said if Horn didn't shut his big mouth, they'd have to send him out of the country. He was sure Horn didn't kill the boy, but not so sure Horn wasn't involved in the attack on the father, and the clubbing of a bunch of his sheep. He also told LeFors, whom he thought he could trust for some reason, that Horn had been paid for other jobs in gold and paper money on a train between Denver and Cheyenne. They talked about getting a job for Horn up in Montana just to get him out of the state before his big mouth got him in trouble."

"Well, I'd appreciate that, Tommy, and I have a question already. Did this feller Prentiss say anything about a letter from a livestock inspector in Montana?"

"How'd you know about that, Angus?"

"Because LeFors told me about it. That was how they got Horn to visit with LeFors in the U.S. Marshals office in Cheyenne. But it wasn't a real job; it was just a ruse to get him to talk."

"And he confessed to get a job? That makes no sense to me."

"I'm not sure at all about this, but I'd say there's a chance he was drunk, or badly hung over. The transcript is clear enough, but as you might know, transcripts have a way of reporting what the interrogator wants said. LeFors played the role of friend and savior to Horn. I expect there will be a big argument over the authenticity of the transcript when the case comes to trial. When I talked to LeFors, I didn't get any notion that the trial would be soon. You hear anything up here about when the trial will be?"

"No, but when it does happen it's gonna be a show of force between some mighty fine lawyers, and a judge who's up for reelection. Have you formed a personal opinion yet?"

"No, not entirely. I can say it looks bad for Horn because the confession was taken with two hidden witnesses, and one of 'em was a court stenographer who wrote it down that same day. That's the transcript. LeFors told me a lot about what's in it, but he would not give me a copy, yet."

"All right, mighty fine," Tommy said, "but here's the thing I wanted to tell you about. You know they held a coroner's inquest starting right there at the Nickell ranch the day after they found the boy's body."

"I knew there was a coroner's inquest, but not sure I knew it was at the father's ranch. I thought it was in Cheyenne."

"We're both right. It started at the Bosler Station—well, actually over at the Nickell Ranch. Then they continued it down in Cheyenne. It was on and off for a good long time. I heard they talked to more 'n a dozen witnesses, including Tom Horn, and members of the Miller and Nickell families."

"Did all the witnesses work either on the Miller ranch or the Nickell ranch? I know they shared a fence line."

"The Miller ranch was several hundred acres, but the old man Nickell only had a quarter-section. Anyhow, there was no love lost between 'em. You know cattle men hate sheep men."

"So, Tommy, there's a transcript of the inquest, right? Know anyone that's read it?"

"I do not, exactly. But there were so many witnesses there and most of 'em live within a half-day's ride of here. And I know a good deal about what some of them said about Horn's movements between various ranches right before and after the morning Willie Nickell was killed. I reckon lots of law men and other interested parties were lookin' to see whether Horn's movements could possibly fix him within shooting distance of that gate where they found the boy's body. I know where different people say they saw Horn about that time. What say you and I ride those same routes and see what we can piece together?"

"Hellavan idea, Tommy. I'm interested in tracking Tom Horn's confession. Maybe the best way to do it is horseback. You lead and I'll pony a pack mule with sleeping rolls and grub if we're gonna be out a while. I brought my .30.40 Winchester with me on the trail. Maybe I'll get a chance to shoot something for dinner."

"Angus, did you know that there's talk about why Tom Horn didn't use a .30.40 instead of his old .30.30?"

"No. What kind of talk?"

"Well, it was a long shot, more 'n three hundred yards. So a .30.40 like yours might have been a better choice—more fire power over long distances. But the talk is Tom Horn preferred his .30.30 on account of he liked to get close up to the man he was shooting at."

"Sounds more like bragging than understanding good gun work, to me. I use a .30.40 because I never want to miss. Got nothing to do with how close, or how far."

CHAPTER 9

T OMMY HAD PIECED together a fair picture of where Tom Horn was at different times just before and soon after Willie Nickel was killed on Thursday, July 18th. Horn had arrived at the Miller ranch on Tuesday, July 15th late in the afternoon. It was common in ranch country for travelers to stop at local ranchers' homes. Apparently, Horn was told to turn his horse out and come in for supper. He slept in the bunkhouse and had breakfast next morning with the Miller family and a young woman boarding there. She was Glendolene Kimmel, the teacher in the little school that was there for a half-dozen small ranches in the Iron Mountain area. She remembered Tom Horn being at the ranch for dinner on Tuesday and most of the next day.

People at the inquest who heard her answer questions said she was well educated and particularly well-spoken. One of the local papers had described her as a most intelligent and interesting witness. She'd told the inquest jurors she was sure Jim Miller and his two boys, Victor and Gus, were home for breakfast on Thursday morning, near the time of Willie Nickell's murder, some three, maybe four miles north of the Miller Ranch. Horn went up to the Nickell's ranch on Wednesday afternoon to see the sheep herd that Nickell had recently purchased in Colorado. They were in what they called the "tree claim," a part of Nickell's property.

Horn had also testified at the Inquest in Cheyenne regarding his whereabouts when Willie Nickel was killed. He said he'd been at the Miller ranch on Tuesday evening, and left there Wednesday morning. Thursday, he'd gone out to a divide between Chug Creek and the Sabylle cabin. He was there Thursday and Friday. That's maybe seven to ten miles away from the Nickell ranch. Said he was doing his job, checking stock for the association, but he was no more 'n a dozen miles away Thursday afternoon. So that's the area that Tommy took Angus to see.

Tommy rode down from Bosler on a new young horse he was turning into a first-class cow horse. It was a gray gelding that looked to be fifteen hands. A nice head, with a good-sized rump.

"Tommy, do I remember correctly that you're more in the horse business than the cow business?"

"Yes, sir, your memory is correct. I'm the cow boss for three small ranches. They run about a hundred grazing steers each on twenty to fifty deeded acres. They use open-range meadows for weight and take their steers to Bosler Station for shipping in the fall. In spring, during the turnout, I move a few hundred head, changing pastures and all. But mostly I buy, board, and raise ranch-broke horses for the big spreads all over southeast Wyoming."

"So, how many horses do you work on a yearly basis?"

"Usually about forty, but in some years, I've moved more from yearlings to two-year-olds. I've got a half-dozen older horses that are too old to work but are still good riding animals. Some ranchers use them on a sort of rental basis for little kids and aged relatives that visit from Kansas and other farming places."

He'd ponied a little easy-keeping dun named Oh-eight, which he said would be just right for Angus. A sensible horse, she had a gray blaze on her face and black feet. He told Angus he could rope off her if it came to that during the next three days.

"We going to be roping horses, or cattle?" Angus asked.

"Probably neither, but in this country you never know. I tied a rope off the saddle horn in case you need it. She won't jump out from under your rope, and she'll let you rope a calf if you need too. I'm think she'll make a fine cutting horse. You ever do much cutting work on a herd, like sorting out unproductive cows from the herd, or sick ones for treatment?"

"No, Tommy. I did some cowboying when I was young, under twenty, but since then I've done most of my riding up on high ridge lines with only my lonesome for company."

"All right then, Angus, let's head north."

He tapped his right spur lightly, and the little gray moved into an easy trot. Angus moved to his right side and kept a lead-rope distance between them. They rode in silence for most of an hour when Tommy pulled up nearly at a fair drop off from the sand and brush down into one of the greenest grasslands Angus had ever seen. It looked deep in small rivulets, creeks, and bogs. Sunny meadows, groves of pine and aspen, with big rocks on the far side of the valley. He could see over five hundred cattle grazing their way up the side of the hill, while a small herd of antelope trotted by as if they owned the place.

"On the far side, sunk down in that draw maybe four miles from here, is the Laramie River," Tommy said. "It runs through Bosler and alongside Laramie City."

CHAPTER 10

A NGUS HAD ALWAYS HEARD that more men, women, and children in Wyoming had been killed by Indians than any other mountain state.

"It was the heart of the Plains Indian country," Tommy explained as they rode. "It was either home or the roving ground for Sioux, Cheyennes, Arapahoes, Shoshones, and Crows. Some said they'd been there so long they thought they owned it. Fact was they did, but it was a right of occupation only. Every Indian there had ancestors from somewhere else; some said it was Old Russia on the other side of Alaska. By the early 1870s, ranchers in southern Montana and northern Wyoming counted on protection from the U.S. Calvary. Their argument was that the Indians migrated here first, but that didn't mean they owned it. It was part of the U.S. now and high time the Indians became civilized and Christians. If they didn't, then the Army would have to get rid of them."

Angus did a little lawman work in Colorado but he was New Mexico bred and born. The takeover by white people was the rule in all three states. But Tommy saw it the way most white ranchers did in Wyoming. He said the way he saw it.

"Well Tommy, I suppose you're right. The whites had bigger guns, more wealth, an army to back 'em up, and a God-given right to take away what the Indians claimed was theirs. It would be a hopeless fight, but the Civil War had the U.S. Army busy in the 1860s. That meant it'd take a few more years before the Indians in Wyoming and Montana would lose their war and purtin' near get wiped out to boot. What's your your take on it?"

"Aw hell, Angus. That was the end of hostilities here in Wyoming, just like it was up north in Montana. What white people called Custer's Last Stand was an armed engagement between the combined forces of the Lakota, Northern Cheyenne, and Arapaho tribes and the 7th Cavalry Regiment of the United States Army."

"What did it have to do with the Tom Horn case down here?"

"Maybe nothing, but I can tell you a little story about a French Canadian farrier, blacksmith, and tin-goods salesman named Augustine Esme. He saw the blood and gore on the battlefield. He was not in the fight, just happened to be a mile away on a high ridge. A year or so later, not sure exactly when, Mr. Esme came down here to Laramie County with his pregnant wife, a Crow woman, and plans to stay awhile. Their first child was born on the banks of the Laramie River just twenty miles north of my ranch in Bosler. They named her Marguerite Esmé. She would spend the next twenty-four years around Bosler going to elementary school, graduating high school in Laramie, and working for the U.S. Postal Service and the Union Pacific Railroad."

"Do you know her?"

"Marguerite was not like everyone else in high school. She doesn't look Indian hardly at all. She spoke English to the other kids, French to her father, and Crow to her mother's family. The girls liked her, the boys loved her, and the teachers tolerated her. Now, she was half-breed, like I said, but most people didn't know that. She was smarter than she was supposed to be. As a girl she was tougher than most boys, and had no respect for what passed as good Christian upbringing. She wore long skirts over heavy boots and rode her own horse to town in the morning, and home to wherever her father's farrier and blacksmithing wagon was."

"You mean she passed for white? With folks here in your home county?"

"Well, whether she passed or it was just folks didn't ask, can't say the truth of that. Her eyes were as black as her hair with something Indian about her cheekbones, but her barely tan skin made her elusive. A few knew her dad was a French Canadian and that made her one too, I suppose. Anyway, she was narrow-hipped, wasp-waisted, and walked with her head high and a confident stride. She wore a beaded pouch over her shoulder every day. Some of the boys thought she had a skinning knife in it."

By the time Angus and Tommy were riding the Bosler area and thinking about Tom Horn, Marguerite had inherited her father's wagon and love of the open range. She was too small, being something short of five feet tall, to be a farrier, so she made a living making and selling things that ranchers needed but couldn't buy at any store in Laramie. Her father had called his big heavy wagon Red Cloud, and he'd taught her how to live as a nomad in a hostile land. Her stout little riding horse, a Morgan named Crazy Horse, followed the wagon night and day. He came at a whistle.

She knew all the stories and had read all the pulp books about the Indian Wars in Montana and Wyoming. Not surprisingly, she took the Indian side of every raid, skirmish, and horse battle. Her mother died when she was ten. The three of them had lived in that wagon since she was born. She lost her father to a drunken bunch of cowboys when she was twelve. They shot him, mistaking him for Sioux, and left his body on the bank of a small creek a few miles near the Horseshoe Road Ranch about forty miles north of Fort Laramie. Marguerite found his body and buried him in a close-by Aspen grove. Then she drove the wagon and team back to Bosler. That was fourteen years ago.

She was twenty-six the day Angus and Tommy George happened on her out on the prairie a few miles north of Bosler Station, five miles from Kels Nickell's ranch.

"What 'n hell is that?" Angus asked when they reached the top of the mountain that marked the center of the Iron Mountain Ranch Company. They were just two miles north of John Coble's place. In between were the James Miller and the William Clay spreads.

"That's the traveling tin-goods store. And not just tin-goods. It has other more mysterious things for sale. That's Marguerite Esme up top, driving the best four-up team of mules in the whole state of Wyoming. That girl can hee and haw a mule team as good as any wagon master in the Rockies. And she will tend to all your needs if she takes a liking to you.

Come on. I'll introduce you. Hell if I know what she knows about Tom Horn, but it will be true if she says it is. Everybody in southeast Wyoming knows about her and is pleased to have her cross their land, 'cept for a few nervous ranch women."

"Why's that?" Angus wondered aloud.

"You'll see when you meet her. She likes young men, won't mingle with ranch wives, and lives in that big ole wagon. That makes her interesting."

"Interesting? What do you mean by that?"

"Well, you'll see she's a fine looker. Short, not taller than five foot, but she's got an hour-glass figure, likes to show it off, and has no inhibitions when it comes to sharing a bunk for a few hours with a man she takes a liking to."

"You saying she's a nighttime woman, a prostitute?"

"Hell no. But she'd be rich if she was. She likes screwing, that's all. But she is careful about who she invites up into her wagon. It's only healthy young men who will enjoy the ride and then leave her in peace with herself. Two young bucka-roos tried to force themselves on her once, when she was bout sixteen. She shot 'em both—with twenty-gauge buckshot. They weren't near dying, or anything like that, but both of 'em were picking buckshot out for the next two summers. She's what church women call promiscuous."

Tommy gave the big bay his head as they switched-backed their way down the steep terrain toward the creek below and the weather-beaten wagon on the well-beaten down road below. He nudged his horse into a trot to move ahead of the wagon. For a few minutes, Angus thought Tommy had changed his mind as they rode past the big wagon a hundred yards up on the side of the hill.

"Best to meet Marguerite head on. Otherwise she might see us as threatening if we ride up behind her. She's got at least two short-barreled shotguns up there under the wagon seat."

Five minutes later they approached her from the front, with Tommy holding his right hand up with a slight wave of his hand.

"Hello, Marguerite, nice to see you again," Tommy said when they closed the gap to shouting distance.

The woman with eight sets of reins threaded through the fingers of both hands tugged back and said something unintelligible to her team. When they came to a stop, she moved both sets of reins to her left hand and notched the brake handle on her right.

"*Bonjour,* Tommy George. *C'est bon de te revoir.*"

Under his breath, Tommy told Angus he thought that was French for nice to see you too. When they pulled up on the side of the wagon seat, Tommy pointed to Angus and said, "I'd like you to meet my friend Angus. Angus, this is Marguerite Esme, and these mules here are a match against any other four-up team in all of Wyoming."

Angus's first thought was the lady might not appreciate being introduced by a description of her mule team, but he smiled and said, "Afternoon, Ma'am, pleasure to meet you."

"I am not a ma'am, *s'il vous plait.* I am but barely twenty-six years of age. I am Mademoiselle Esme, and you are Mr. Angus what? Monsieur George failed to say your last name."

"Name's Angus, Mademoiselle Esme. I have a last name, but it's hard on the tongue so everyone just calls me Angus," he said, still with a smile.

"Perhaps some other time you will tell me your proper last name, and I'll pronounce it in French for you. My father's native tongue softens every word, and maybe it will do so for your hard last name. Now, Tommy, my friend, is there anything you need from my wagon? If so, perhaps you and your friend would like to join me for a mid-day *vin et fromage*."

Angus has no idea what she said, but ten minutes later, when they'd watered their horses in the creek and walked back to the rear of the huge wagon, he understood. The rear of the eight-foot tall wagon had a drop-down table. Marguerite had pulled the rubber-stopper on a bottle of pink wine, sliced a half-dozen pieces of a yellow cheese ring, and produced a small basket of broken hunks of bread. She poured three small cups of wine, and handed one to him, one to Tommy, and lifted hers in their direction.

"*Toast de vin français*," she said, with a slight curve at the sides of her mouth. Not quite a smile, Angus thought, but not a frown either.

"Here's looking at you," Tommy answered as he sipped from the edge of the small blue cup.

"Mighty fine," Angus said, as he emptied his little cup. "Never drank wine out of a cup before. Mighty fine, I'd say."

They each took a slice of cheese. Tommy smiled. Angus nearly gagged. It was as foul tasting as anything he'd had ever tried, but he swallowed it anyhow. Tommy and Marguerite exchanged weather and road information, then switched to water, grass, and horseflesh. Turns out Marguerite loved mules in front of her wagon but hated riding them. They're working animals, not fit to ride, she said without further explanation.

As she talked, never looking directly at him, Angus tried to figure out what made her so striking.

Her face, a light olive color, was sharp-featured, almost chiseled, and showed no movement when she talked. She never raised her thin eyebrows, and he could detect no furrows on her forehead. She kept her head still and didn't nod or shake her head in almost five minutes of conversation. Her black shiny eyes seemed to talk for her as they glowed and glistened through the mundane conversation. She'd asked Tommy what his friend was doing in Wyoming. Tommy said he was here for horses. Frowning for the first time, she asked Tommy a question as though Angus was not standing right there at the drop-down table with them.

"Your friend, Angus, bereft of a last name, is here to do what? Buy or sell horses? Is that what you meant when you said he was looking at your horse operations here in Laramie County?"

"Well, not exactly, Marguerite," Tommy said. Then he told her the little fiction they'd worked out to explain why a stranger was riding with Tommy and asking questions about Tom Horn.

"Angus has his own horse ranch in the Espanola Valley in New Mexico, but that's pretty dry country, winter and summer, down there, so he might bring up twenty or so head next summer on the train. To Bosler. To my horse ranch."

"Okay if I call you Marguerite?" Angus interrupted.

"*Qui*, of course," she said.

"I'm here for two reasons," said Angus, "One is finding a place where I can work maybe two dozen young horses and

still put weight on 'em in the process. I train roping and cutting horses for small ranches that don't do their own breaking
on round-up stock. But they need to grow from nine hundred
pounds to about twelve-hundred pounds during their second
summer as colts and fillies. The grass up here is mighty fine,
like the wine you poured for us. The other reason I'm here
has to do with Tom Horn, and his troubles with the law. I'm
a part-time deputy U.S. marshal in Colorado, working special
cases for Marshal Ramsey in Denver. He's interested in Tom
Horn, so since I wanted to come up here anyway to look into
pasturing some horses this summer, he obliged me with a
train ticket and five dollars a day, federal salary. Wondering
if you've ever met the man. Tom Horn, I mean."

Marguerite leaned away from the table and brushed a speck
of breadcrumb from her left sleeve. Her black hair cascaded
over one shoulder, and she gestured to answer his question.

"Met him? Yes, I've met him. I've entertained him too, if
that's what you're asking about. He's a man of substance. A
killer, but just one of many in this violent place I love so much.
He brags more than he kills. He did his job, a stock detective
he called it, by growing his reputation by word of mouth as
much as by firing his .30.30 long-barrel rifle. And he is feared,
without being fearful. What does your Marshal Ramsey want
to know? Did he kill that fourteen-year old boy—or does it
matter? He's guilty by reputation and will likely hang by his
reticence. Know him. Yes, I know him."

Tommy seemed astounded. "Well, if that don't take all.
Marguerite, I should have known that you and Tom Horn
were friends. He's been roaming this country for years now,
mostly by himself. Now that I think on it, of course you'd

know him. I share your notion that his reputation rides out in front of him like a team of draft horses hauling a freight wagon up a steep grade. Are you in a hurry to get to Bosler before dark? If not, I'm thinking that Angus and me would love to have a creek-side dinner with you this fine evening. We've got cold-wrapped venison steaks and two bottles of decent whiskey. Might that be possible? We'd camp on the other side of the creek, so our snoring during the night don't bother you none."

Angus and Tommy walked their horses across the creek and unsaddled them. Angus said he'd do the brushing. Tommy went back across the creek and offered to water Marguerite's mules. She apparently said yes because Tommy took them, two at a time, downstream to water.

Marguerite started a small cook fire, settled a grill on it, and made biscuits on the drop-down table. Tommy grilled the venison; Marguerite baked the biscuits and cut more cheese— a different kind with a pleasing rather than a pungent smell. She opened a tin of canned peaches and drew fresh cold water from the creek. They ate standing up and then settled down on logs around the cook fire. Angus found enough dead tree branches to last several hours, and they sat by the fire, drinking whiskey.

"I guess I met Tom Horn about four years ago," Tommy offered. "There was a dinner hosted by John Coble at his ranch. He introduced Horn as a great cowboy who'd won prizes in bull dogging and calf roping at the Wyoming Stampede two years earlier. Said he was going to help the big ranches with their cattle-rustling problem. Seemed a quiet man, but not one you could trifle with. When did you first meet him, Marguerite?"

"Maybe a year or a year and a half ago. He rode up to my wagon one morning, just as I was putting my mules into their traces. My lead mule had a stone bruise in the frog of her foot. He spotted it right off. Took care of it too, with some salve he had in his saddlebag. We talked for a while. He's not well educated, but he is well read. He wondered if I'd sell him a bag of coffee—said he'd run out two days earlier. 'Two days without coffee?' I asked him, knowing all cowboy's addiction to caffeine. 'Whiskey makes up for it,' he said, with that grin he only gives to young girls out on the prairie. My assessment of him differs with yours, Tommy. Yes, he was quiet, but he was definitely a man you could trifle with. I expect he'd been trifling with women all his life. That's how he struck me from the beginning."

Tommy went quiet. Angus took the trifle talk in. Did she mean what he thought she meant?

"Well," Angus said, "you both have the advantage over me. I never met him. But I've talked to a good many that have, and I think you're both right. Tom Horn's friends, well-wishers, detractors, and those he crossed all said he was frank, temperate when sober, and could be trusted to do whatever job a man needed done. He had little patience for the slumbering of the law and no forgiveness for anyone that stole anything. He hated thieves more than anything else in his world. He never had children or much of a family life. But no one, until Willie Nickell got murdered, ever thought he had it in him to shoot a young boy."

"What do you think, Mr. Angus? Are you investigating the case, or just interested in it?"

"I don't know what to think. My experience with the law is that most men don't confess to murder unless they did murder. What people say about a man doesn't' count for much in a courtroom. But a confession shouts out guilt like a thunderstorm starts a stampede. If he had not confessed, no jury would hang him even if they thought he was a hired killer of cattle rustlers, without taking them in for trial. But I'm keen to hear your sense of it, Marguerite."

"My sense of it? Of what—his confession—or his guilt—or his innocence? By sense, are you asking what I know, or what I sense? I sense things every day without knowing they actually happened. If it's raining, and the rain turns to sleet, I know it's cold; I'm not guessing at it. Sensing something is a feeling, not a confirmation. Tom Horn is a man of his word—I believe that. When I'm around him, I feel safe. I sense that. I don't know for a fact that he killed Willie Nickell. I doubt it. And because I doubt he killed the boy, I doubt he confessed to it. My sense of it, based on maybe three or four visits, is he was tricked into saying things that now look like a confession but really aren't. I think he is a danger to the ranchers who turned him loose out on the prairie to kill bad men. Wyoming will forgive them and him for that. But if they believe his confession, Wyoming will hang him. It doesn't matter whether he did it or not. All that matters is they *say* he admitted it. I don't believe it because I don't believe his confession."

Tommy, sipping on his whiskey, kicked a small piece of burning log back into the fire. All three turned quiet, enjoying the night, and the wonder that always comes from watching a campfire up close.

"You know," Tommy said, "there's a piece of this that no one wants to talk about. What if Tom Horn was there, on orders from John Coble, to shoot Kels Nickell, and he mistook the boy for the father? Might that explain why he confessed? Maybe he can't admit his mistake, but can't abide the fact he shot an innocent boy?"

Marguerite shook her head. "Well, I've read all the papers, a few days late as usual, but they kept saying the word premeditation. They say he did it on purpose. Does it matter if you killed the wrong person? Is a mistake a defense?"

Angus was never accused of being lawyerlike, but he'd arrested enough suspects to know the basics. He tried to settle Marguerite's worries about her sometimes friend, Tom Horn. "If you point a loaded rifle at someone with the intent to kill 'em, but you miss and hit somebody else standing close by, it's still first-degree murder. Missing is no defense. Hitting the wrong person is no defense."

"OK, that settles it for me," she retorted. "From everything Tom Horn ever told me, he doesn't miss. He hits what he aims at. He brags about it. And he's always sure when he aims a gun. He could not have been aiming at the father and hit the son. That'd be missing the father. What the newspapers don't talk about is why he would want to kill Kels Nickell over sheep. John Coble and his big ranching friends didn't hire Tom Horn to keep sheep out; they hired him to get rid of cattle rustlers. That's why I don't believe he was there in the first place. Kels Nickel was an angry man—so was his neighbor James Miller. They'd been at one another for years."

Angus reminded them he was the only one at the campfire who had never talked to Tom Horn.

"Well, could be, but I've talked to the prosecutors, and they say Horn was in the area and could have done it. He's got no alibi to prove he wasn't there at the Nickell gate the morning the boy was shot. They didn't charge him until they got his confession. That's why he's in jail waiting for trial. It's not because he could have done it; it's because he said he did it."

Next morning, when the false dawn appeared and Angus's lifelong habit of getting up before sunrise kicked in, he took the little dun back down to the creek for water. Marguerite was up and stepping her mules into their traces. He thought about walking over to her side and offering to help. Then he thought better of it. She was gone before he and Tommy finished their morning coffee.

As they rode to Bosler Station, Angus said with a grin, "Tommy, it comes to me that the age difference between Tom Horn and Marguerite is about the same as the difference between you and Marguerite. She entertained Horn a few times in that big old wagon of hers. Did she ever invite you in?"

Tommy and Angus had joshed one another on things like horses, bad habits, too much whiskey, and women over the last three days. So he was taken aback at Tommy's answer.

"Angus, there's some things a man is not disposed to talk about. Visiting young women out on the prairie is one of 'em. Let's just keep it that way."

CHAPTER 11

O N AUGUST 4, 1901, just seventeen days after Willie Nickell was killed, terror again struck the Nickell family. The *Cheyenne Daily Leader* sensationalized the story the next day in its glaring headline on the top of page one. **"EXTERMINATION OF A WHOLE FAMILY."** The subtitle explained: **"KELS NICKELL, FATHER OF WILL NICKELL, WHO WAS MURDERED A SHORT TIME AGO, THE OBJECT OF A THRILLING ATTEMPT TO KILL BY TWO HIDDEN SLAYERS—LEFT ARM BROKEN IN AN ASSAULT NEAR HIS RANCH—TWELVE SHOTS FIRED FROM AMBUSH."**

The newspaper, written and published seventy miles away from the Nickell's ranch in Albany County, had details, some of which were accurate. "Yesterday morning twelve shots were fired from magazine guns by two men in ambush at Kels Nickell within three hundred yards of his ranch." Some guns at the turn of the 19th century had magazines to hold cartridges, but there was no such thing as a magazine gun. The newspaper assumed the shooting was done "by two men in ambush" and that the shots were fired less than three hundred yards from the intended victim. During the next few days, the actual facts were coughed up by deputies from both Laramie and Albany counties.

Turns out multiple shots were fired, but the exact number was unclear. Kels was out milking his cows at 6 am that Sunday morning. Two men, far away, had fired in rapid succession. One bullet hit his left elbow. Others spattered all around him as he ran back into his house. He was sure one bullet made a stinging and smarting sensation across his right hip. Another glanced across his back. Kels told everyone he was positive about who the two men were that attacked him, but he wouldn't tell the reporters their names. When Laramie County deputies showed up, he said the two men were Jim Miller and one of his sons.

When Tommy and Angus reined in their horses on top of a mesa overlooking the Kels ranch, Tommy filled Angus in on the second shooting on that ranch.

"Way I hear it, Angus, they reconvened the coroner's inquest in Cheyenne."

Angus, shaking his head asked, "Reconvened? You mean they reconvened the coroner's request about the boy's shooting because his father got shot?"

"That's the way I heard it but . . ."

"Hellfire, Tommy, something's wrong about Wyoming law. You can't have a coroner investigating a shooting where a man's arm got broke. He's the coroner—he's called when the shooting is fatal, not just wounding a man. And besides, the man with the broken arm said it was two men firing at him and he knew who they were. He named them, and neither one was called Tom Horn. That's outside both the law and the facts in the Tom Horn case."

"Maybe so, but Angus, I was in town that week buying two colts and a young filly to turn out on my pasture. Two shootings in my backyard were of some interest to me. So I sat in the back of the room for that reconvening, listening to the testimony. Course, I knew most all the witnesses and three or four of the jurors. I was a mite surprised when the prosecutor, Mr. Stoll, expanded the hearing on the dad's shooting to take more evidence on the boy's shooting. Hell, they even connected both shootings to antagonism all over the Iron Mountain range toward sheep owners. Kels Nickell, old fool that he was, had brought near three thousand head of sheep."

"Why'd he do that? I thought he was a rancher," Angus asked.

"He is a rancher, but he hates the Miller brand, and they run a lot more cows than he did. So, some say, he did it just to spite old man Miller and his no-account boys. That's the Nickell view, anyhow. I know Jim Miller and his older son, Gus. They are good folks, but they sure got a bug up about Kels and his kin."

"How'd it turn out? The reconvened coroner's inquest, I mean."

"Took two more days. They called all the members of the Nickell family, including Julia Nickell Cook. She's Willie's older sister. Her testimony was dramatic. Kels left the house early to milk cows. She and Bill Mahoney, Kels brother, heard six shots, loud and clear. The whole family streamed out of the house and toward the barn just as Kels came running toward them. They saw him running right through the potato patch on the east side of the house. They helped Kels stumble his way back onto the porch. The way she put it, the men in the house were afraid to go outside to harness the coach horses, so she saddled a horse and rode four miles to the Reed ranch. A couple hours later they got Kels in a wagon and took him to town for treatment of his broke arm. Now here's where her testimony got interesting. She said her father did not tell the family who shot him. Kels's wife, Mary, said the same thing."

"What made that interesting?"

"Because Kels himself told the coroner's jury he was sure it was Jim Miller and one of his boys. Sort of casts doubt on Kels's testimony, don't it? And there was another witness who was interesting—Victor Miller, Jim Miller's youngest son. Remember, this all happened on a Sunday morning. Most ranch families were gathered at the grandparents' houses. Victor Miller was at home that morning and he went to a close neighbor's house, the McDonalds, and told them someone had shot Mr. Nickell. That got Walter Stoll's attention. He asked how Victor could have known about the attack so early on the morning it happened. Victor had an explanation—involving a string of people. Remember that Julia Nickell rode to the Reed ranch for help. Joe Reed was riding to the Nickell ranch when he met up with Gus Miller, Jim's older son. He told Gus that Mr. Nickell had been shot. Gus rode back home to his family ranch, four miles away, and told his family about the shooting."

Angus reined up a little and stretched out his right leg from the stirrup. He wagged his boot some and the rowel on his spur tinkled.

"So, Tommy, I take it you know those Miller boys, right? What are they like?"

"I know 'em, but not real well. I can say Victor struck me when he was testifying as polite and straight up about what he saw and heard. Gus was a little wild sometimes, but all in all, they were good boys, I'd say."

"Was there any testimony about who might have shot the old man, Kels?"

"Two of the Nickell girls, one named Trixie and the other Margaret, or Maggie, said they'd seen two horses riding away. They didn't know the men on 'em, but Trixie said the horses looked like ones she seen at the Miller ranch. One was a bay and the other sort of an iron gray. Fred Nickell saw them too, but didn't' say who the men were or the color of the horses they rode. He did say they were headed in the same direction as the Miller ranch, which borders the Nickell ranch, you know."

"Sounds like the evidence was pointing clear as stream water at the Miller boys."

"Maybe, but Joe Reed's testimony messed that up. He said he had gone out and tried to confirm what the Nickell girls had said but could not find any horse tracks where the men were supposed to have ridden. He'd asked around and no one else said anything about a bay and a gray and two men riding away from the Nickell ranch toward the Miller Ranch. I think the jury discarded the girl's testimony because Trixie was nine and Maggie was about seven."

"So how'd the jury find on the case?"

"The talk was mostly about Joe Reed's testimony and the fact that Kels himself never identified the Miller boys until after he spent that Sunday in town getting medical treatment. Joe Reed is your picture book image of a Wyoming cattle rancher. Besides, he's the one that rode at a full gallop to the Nickell's ranch right after an ambush had occurred. He thought nothing about his own safety—that alone made him a credible witness."

At the end of two days of testimony, the coroner's jury made no findings in either the killing of Willie Nickell or his father's attack. Prosecutor Walter Stoll spent a day discounting rumors about a $500 payment by Jim Miller to anyone who'd agree to shoot Kels Nickell, or about a man named Bill Edwards being offered $1000 to kill Kels Nickell, or a connection between the attacks on both father and son, or last, about seeing Miss Glendolene Kimmell riding a horse around Albany County with Tom Horn.

Tommy and Angus rode the last two miles to the Nickell ranch in silence. When they topped out on a small hill facing the wide plain below, Angus opened a new subject.

"You know there's a lot of sheep ranching going on in Colorado now. But you're telling me Wyoming has not taken to sheep."

"Angus, you are right. Wyoming doesn't take to sheep like our southern neighbor does. Cattle is king here. The ranchers, especially the big ones, believe right down to the bottom of their boots that Wyoming's grasslands belong to them and sheep will kill the cattle industry because they destroy the grass. What makes it worse is Colorado being the source for sheep being brought up here by rail car. Kels bought three thousand head of sheep from Loveland, Colorado. A man named John Schroder drove 'em up here from the railyards. One witness at the inquest said he knew for sure that John Schroder was told by a man just south of Bosler that Kels would not live to see 1902 if he puts sheep on his land."

"Was it his land he put the sheep on?" Angus asked.

"Some of the time, but also on the public domain used by every rancher in Albany County. In fact, John Schroder himself testified at the inquest and confirmed the first man's story. Another witness said Kels told him he was 'going to eat up his neighbor's pasture and that by the time his sheep got done there wouldn't be enough grass to feed a grasshopper.'"

Angus slapped his gloved right hand down hard onto his chaps.

"Whowee! I expect every cowman in the courtroom bristled at that. You know this Kels, right? Does he have some kind of death wish?"

"No, but ornery does not near describe Kels Nickell when it comes to his feud with Jim Miller. He's cross as a bear and meaner than a skunk in a bedroll."

"So what happened? Did he let 'em feed on public domain land?"

"He did. They stray down from his ranch onto public land between his place and Miller's. They're close to some of John Coble's holdings as well. Just because he was an ornery old cuss, Kels boasted about his sheep causing a big Goddamn stir with every cattleman in the county."

"Did Tom Horn know about Kels Nickell's sheep?"

"Yep, he sure did. He told the coroner's jury he'd reported the presence of sheep on Miller's 'tree claim.'"

"Tree claim? What's that?"

"Not sure. I took it to be one of Jim's pastures. That was two days before Willie was killed. And to make it worse, just one day before Kels himself was attacked, the Millers discovered those sheep had come right down the hill to their garden. Now there's a question here because the land Miller was using for pasture was actually government land he'd fenced in. But the garden was on Miller's deeded land. There was a threat made to Kels's sheepherder, a man named Vingenjo Biango."

"Did the prosecutor, Walter Stoll, call the sheepherder to the stand?"

"Yeah, but I'd left by then. Later, I heard he told the jury something about a man screaming at him and saying, 'I'll fix that son of a bitch before morning!' That was on Saturday; Kels was attacked Sunday morning. It gets worse. This man Biango also testified that the morning of the attack, Kels was getting ready to be taken to town for treatment of his broken arm. He sent for Biango, gave him a rifle and ten dollars. Two hours later, Biango said a man and two boys on horseback came back to the sheep pasture. They scared him so he went down the hill and hid behind a big rock. They started firing at him, thirty shots, he said. But he told the jury he did not know them but that 'he did notice them sufficiently to see.' But other witnesses contradicted the sheepherder's story. Stoll decided the man had too many inconstancies and too much trouble expressing himself in English, so he wasn't a convincing witness."

"That the end of it?"

"No. There's no doubt that a lot of Kels's sheep were shot and killed and that whoever did that also scared the beejeezus out of that poor sheepherder. He left Albany County. Joe Reed confirmed that a lot of sheep were crippled and killed. Reed said he counted between fifty and sixty, but there could have been eighty. Joe LeFors came to the Nickell ranch later that afternoon and said he found twenty-five or thirty carcasses. Oh, did I tell you about the teacher, Elizabeth Stein?"

"No, you told me about a teacher named Glendolene Kimmell. You said she didn't want to confirm how many Millers were having breakfast at the Miller ranch house the morning Willie Nickel was killed. I think you said last night she didn't think it was honorable to convey information about the family because she was a boarder in their house, and whose children she taught at the little school on their land."

"Right, but this is a different teacher. Miss Stein testified that the shooting of Kels was not unexpected. She said everyone around Bosler thought the bullet was meant for the father the first time, and that they meant to get Kels sometime."

"Dang. That's pretty powerful testimony," Angus said. "Women, especially educated ones like teachers, usually speak for a whole community."

"Suppose you're right, but after hearing from several dozen witnesses, the coroner's jury came up empty handed. Lots of hints and opinions, but no clear line of evidence leading to Tom Horn in Willie Nickell's murder, or to Jim Miller and his boys in the Kels Nickell attack."

"All right then. I wonder if the other teacher, Miss Kimmell, would mind talking to me about Tom Horn and Willie Nickell. Is she still the teacher there?"

"No, she's not. Someone said she was fixing to leave the state. But she might still be in Laramie City. We could check on that after we take a look at the killing site. It's only four miles away. It'll be dark by the time we get there. What say we camp down there on the south bank of that pretty little creek? We'll build us a nice fire, cook those last two venison steaks, and maybe have a drink of whiskey."

CHAPTER 12

THEY SCRAPED OUT a little fire pit twenty yards from the rippling water of the North Chugwater Creek. Didn't take long to cook dinner or have a couple tin cups with whiskey and coffee. Once they settled on opposite sides of the campfire, Angus asked Tommy what he knew for sure about Kels Nickell.

"I know a little in person and more by range gossip. Sold him a horse two summers ago. Listened to him rant about the Millers in particular and the other ranchers who had sizeable herds on public land all over this county. He's an ornery cuss, as I think I mentioned earlier. But his boys and his daughters didn't seem to take after him. They were more like their mother, Mary. Can't say I know her well, but I had supper at their house two or three times in the last five years. Nice woman, I'd say. What else you want to know?"

"Seems to me, Tommy, that the father of the boy must have played some role in the unfortunate fact his son was murdered. Got any ideas on what the role might be?"

"Well, I don't have much first-hand, but everyone in Iron Mountain country knows the history of everybody else. Kels is a homesteader, more of a farmer than a rancher, and has a mighty fine history behind him. I remember the bartender at the Laramie Hotel telling us one night that Kels was an Indian fighter as a young man up north of here—in both Wyoming and Montana. They said he rode in General George C. Crook's command."

"You mean back fifteen years ago when George Armstrong Custer got his whole troop ambushed by Red Cloud and Crazy Horse at the Little Big Horn? All of those soldiers were part of General Crook's command."

"Can't say he was there. You know you just can't come out and ask a man about a defeat like that. But the bartender was sure Kels was with Crook at the Battle of the Rosebud just north of Sheridan, Wyoming. I think that was just a few days before Custer's annihilation."

"Where is Kels from, before he soldiered with Gen. Crook?"

"Kentucky, I think. He came here after enlisting with the U.S. Army in the 1880s. He was stationed with the horse cavalry at Fort Laramie, I'd say probably about twenty years ago. When he mustered out and married up, he filed his homestead in the Iron Mountain Region, just four miles north of us right now."

"What was the homesteading fee back then, you know?"

"My grandfather paid $1.25 an acre for his 480 acres. But he sold a lot of it to ranchers more than twenty years ago. My piece—just eighty acres—was part of that original homesteading claim. It's on the same creek we're camping on right now. But you asked about Kels, not me. I'll say this. Kels had a dynamite temper, but he was never shy about hard work—the

Army—the homesteading—the sheep. You'll meet him in the morning. He's got steely eyes and some would say he's a handsome man. Fancies a sizeable drooping mustache, but no other face hair. Keeps his collar buttoned at all times—expect that's a carryover from his trooper days. And there was a time when he got along with his closest neighbor, Jim Miller."

"Got along? I thought they'd been feuding a long time, and near hated one another."

"That's the case now, but some years ago both families worked to build the little school located halfway between their homes. All the kids from both families were schooled there, with Miss Kimmell being the latest teacher. Her teaching wage is paid by both families, and the Millers give her board and food. Now that you remind me of it, John Coble has a role with all three. As you know, he hired Tom Horn as a stock detective in this area. Coble's main ranch—he has several—but the main one borders the west side of Nickell's homestead. Sometime earlier this year, Coble's foreman, a man named George Cross, got into a fight over cattle with Kels. Somehow, Coble also got involved, and Kels ended up cutting Coble pretty good with a knife. Coble sided with Jim Miller. So, Kels hated them all, probably Tom Horn too."

"You saying Kels knew Tom Horn?"

"Ain't gonna say that, but Tom Horn rode this country all the time. Probably was in and out of the North Chugwater Creek hundreds of times. Most likely watered his horse out of the Laramie River more times than we could count."

Next morning, two hours after sunrise, Tommy and Angus wound their way along the creek and then across a half-dozen pastures, most with gates, which they were careful to shut behind them. They came to a well-traveled road that led to a single train track mounded up on both sides and topped by oil-drenched ties holding fast to the single track. No sign or sound of a train. A two-hour ride took them to the gate.

"This is it," Tommy said.

"Where the boy was shot?" Angus asked.

"They said at the inquest that he was most likely trying to close the gate when the first bullet struck him in the left armpit. That bullet exited through his chest. The second shot hit him as he turned and wound down and out near his hip bone. Hard to believe, but the docs and the folks who found his body the next morning said he ran about sixty-five feet back toward the house before he collapsed on the road, right down there."

"I can't see their house, but am I remembering right that it's less than a mile?" Angus asked.

"You are. Most everyone in the house heard three shots but took them for someone out hunting. They knew it was up the road, but that didn't tell them something was amiss."

"And the shots were fired from where, up there, on the side of the big hill?"

"Damn straight," Tommy said, as he edged his horse to the gate, leaned over, and un-looped it, swinging the wire gate in with him as he rode into the Nickell Ranch. There was no sign, but most folks in the Bosler area knew which gate led to which family for miles around. Angus neck-reined the bay, followed Tommy in, and dismounted.

"Suppose it's OK to stay here a minute? I'd like to maybe walk up there and get a look at what the shooter could see. It was a three-hundred yard shot, right?"

"Suppose so, but maybe we ought to just ride down to the house first. Wouldn't want to introduce you to Kels, up here on his land, without announcing our presence at the house first."

Angus nodded and mounted the bay; they trotted down the road to the Kels ranch buildings. The main house was what you'd expect for a fairly well-to-do homestead. The L-shaped house was of cut logs, about a foot-square, with wide sets of plastered mud in between. There was a large door on the bottom leg and two-foot-wide windows along both faces of the house. The north end had a wood fence strung out for maybe forty feet, enclosing a large vegetable garden. The front dirt was well tamped down and looked raked. One big stone chimney stuck up on the south end of the house and a smaller tin-pipe was on what was probably the kitchen on the near side of the house.

There was a covered porch leading to an oversized door. Kels was sitting there on a pine rocking chair with a rifle settled across his legs.

"Morning, Tommy," he said, holding his jaw taut and without moving his eyes or any part of his body.

"Kels," Tommy said, and nodded to Kels as they slow walked their horses to about fifteen feet from the house. "I've got a new friend with me," he added as both men loosened their reins to a loop, and both horses came to stand still.

"You boys here on business, or just passing by?" Kels asked.

"Bit of both, Kels, bit of both. I'd like to introduce you to a Colorado man. His name is Angus. He's a horse rancher like me, and we're talking over some horse-trading we might do next summer. But he's got an interest in Tom Horn too. And so that's the business part. Mind if we dismount, or would you rather we'd just go right back out your gate?"

"Ah, hell, Tommy. Just get down. Let's go inside. Coffee's gone, but Mary will get us some spring water. We can talk inside."

During the next hour, Kels answered questions with few words. But he also staked out his position on Tom Horn.

"Mr. Angus, I'll accept your condolences over the killing of my boy, and I wish you good luck in helping the Colorado law men make their own charges against him. But there's a mighty big hole in the thinking up here about Mr. Horn. He's the one that killed my boy, there's no doubt about that. But the hole in the thinking up here is did Tom Horn also shoot me, and kill damn near a hundred of my sheep? The law is confused about that. So, let me ask you plain out. Are you looking into who shot me, or is your interest just in what killing Tom Horn did down in Colorado?"

"Mr. Nickell," Angus said slowly, taking in a breath, "I'm a nearly full-time horse rancher and barely a part-time deputy U.S. marshal in Colorado. My boss in Denver is only interested in the conduct of Tom Horn. Best as I can tell, the case against Horn for killing your boy is looped and tied with a pigging string by his own confession to Deputy LeFors. I met with LeFors in his Cheyenne office just a week ago. He firmly believes in Horn's guilt based on his confession and other aspects of the case. He expressed no opinion on whether Horn shot you or killed your sheep. My instructions are to make inquiries into the man's criminal activities up here only as far as they might impact a case that's been filed down in Colorado."

"Mr. Angus, can't say as I am following you. It's like an antelope jumping fences, streams, and downed logs. First, you're talking about Horn killing my boy, but then you jumped to whether Colorado might try him for something he did there. I lost your track."

"Sorry, Mr. Nickell. Can't blame you for that. The assistant attorney general in Denver told me that they have grand jury indictments against Horn for criminal conduct in Colorado. If Horn is convicted up here and gets the death sentence, then Colorado likely won't extradite him down there for trial. But if he gets a prison sentence here, then they will consider a trial against him in Colorado. I'm here to follow the legal proceedings, but I'm also taking a look at Mr. George's horse ranch operation. We have business interests in common."

"All right, I'm understanding the situation now. So, here's the nub of it. Horn is probably the one that shot my boy Willie. I'll say it plain out. When he lined Willie out, he thought he was aiming at me. He bore no grudge against me and his bosses never instructed him to shoot my boy. I was the target, not Willie. Horn shot a boy thinking he was a man. Damn fool. But he ain't the one that shot me. That was Jim Miller and his boys, or at least one of his boys. That's plain truth. But there's others, whose opinions are suspect to me, who say Horn did not kill my boy. I say suspect because Horn is being protected, with good lawyers, by the cattlemen who hate me because I'm a sheep man. Hell, the Miller bunch hate me for other reasons, too. I'm a homesteader and they hate that. I'm for access to public land for everyone; they're for using it to graze their cattle, and to hell with everyone else. But far as I can tell, John Coble and his friends never told Horn to come after me, or kill my sheep. That's on the son of a bitch name of James Miller."

With that, Kels told Tommy and Angus they were welcome to ride his ranch and talk to any of his family or hands they wanted to. They said their thanks to Mary for the cold spring water, mounted up, and rode back up to the gate to take a better look at the terrain.

At the gate, they dismounted and ground tied their horses. Tommy gave Angus a short tale of what a half-dozen lawmen found on the morning after Willie's body was found.

"Angus, as you can see, the slope up there from where we're standing is a mix of rock-outcroppings, pine trees, some oak brush, and a fair pitch upward to the thicker forest on top of the ridge. Now, look over the other side of the fence, where I'm pointing. Do you see that rock outcropping about three hundred yards from here? There's a thirty-foot pine and scrub oak sticking out around the outcropping. That's where the deputies and neighbors who were the first to come here the day after the shooting think the shooter was lying in wait."

"Yes, sir, I see it. It raises more questions than it answers. First one being who the shooter lying in wait was trying to kill."

Tommy shook his head. "Goddamn, Angus! The shooter was lying in wait for Kels, of course. Who'd want to shoot a fourteen-year-old boy?"

"That raises a barrel full of questions. Did the fourteen-year-old boy look anything like a man? Did he ride a horse like his dad? Maybe it was his dad's horse. The deputies said he took his time—opened the gate, dismounting on the other side, walking back to close the gate. What happened to his horse? Could he see the rock outcropping? If so, did he get a look at the shooter? What made him come back to the gate? Did he have his back to the shooter? Is that why the bullets hit him on the left side? I mean, there's a lot the deputies didn't cover."

Tommy went quiet. Then, after looking up at the rocks and back at the gate area, he shook his head up and down.

"All right Angus, the first men to come up here the next morning were all family. They were in shock. The next people were neighbors, not deputies or detectives of any kind. The deputies knew it was a boy killed, and I suppose they assumed the shooter knew it was a boy, at least at first, and . . ."

"At first. Think about that, Tommy. If the shooter knew it was a boy before he fired the first shot, then Kels was damn sure not the intended victim. Unless of course the shooter fired in haste, not taking the time to make sure it was a man, or not a man. If the shooter was either Jim Miller or one of his boys, isn't it likely they would easily tell the difference between Kels and Willie? But if the shooter was Tom Horn, maybe he would not have readily recognized the boy from the man."

"Angus, you're talking like a detective but you're talking to a cowboy. Hell if I know one way or the other."

"Yeah, Tommy, I know, but I'm asking questions out loud to get them out of my head. I can understand the family not paying much attention to the distance or that big rock up there. But when the law arrived, they should have been asking the same questions I'm pondering out loud. Seems from what you told me about the testimony there was more speculating going on here than there was in the silver boom down in Leadville, Colorado, twenty years ago."

"Well, if they found silver in a town called Leadville, they may have missed some clues down there too."

Tommy and Angus sort of switch-backed their way up the rocky hill to the big pine growing on the far side. As they walked, Angus continued his one-sided conversation. "OK, Willie stopped at the gate and dismounted. We know that because he was afoot at the gatepost when he was first hit. My guess is the shooter didn't much care whether he shot a boy or a man. It's the same message, boy or man; if it was Horn—don't bring in sheep. But if it was Jim Miller or his boys, it's a different message. You see, the boy didn't brink in sheep—only his father. So, where's that leave us?"

"In doubt, Tommy said, like everyone else."

"I talked at some length with Deputy LeFors and his boss. They were damn sure about the shooter being Horn long before he confessed; if in fact he did confess. That's mostly because of the rock the shooter put under the boy's head once he was down and probably bleeding out. That, they said, was Horn's calling card. That's how he built his reputation and that's how he got paid."

When they reached the outcropping, they went to the back so they could see downslope at the fence, the gate, and their horses.

"How long would you say it took us to get here from the gate?"

"Dunno," Tommy said, "maybe five, six minutes."

Angus fished out his railroader's watch from his vest. "No, it took eleven minutes. That's not bad wearing chaps, spurs, and walking uphill for three hundred yards. Do you agree we have a clear look at the horses, the gate, and the road back down to the Nickell ranch house?"

"Sure, it's clear for I'd say a quarter mile."

"So the shooter had a good long look at the boy riding his horse from a quarter mile off. Right?"

"He did."

"Do you see anything different about that horse you let me ride? Anything different about the saddle or the tack?"

"Well, now that you ask, there's something red tied to the saddle horn. That's different. You put that there?"

"I did. It's my handkerchief. See how easy it is to see from here? Little thing like a handkerchief. Clear as a bell, right?"

"It is."

"The shooter had a clear view, for a long way, for a long time. He took his time sighting in his victim. Why did he wait for the dismount? Was he uncertain about who it was? Did he have time to think about what he was about to do? And once he fired three quick shots, why did he go all the way down there and put a rock under a fourteen-year old boy's head?"

"Angus, you're getting at something. Instead of asking me questions, how about you just tell me what you're thinking?"

"I'm thinking the shooter knew damn well that it was a boy he was sighting in, not a man. He had a long look, and that red handkerchief tied to the saddle horn is clearly visible at this distance. Kels is a tall man, and he's getting on in age a little. He would sit a horse different than a young boy would. He would not dismount to open or close a gate, like the boy did. This whole affair tells me the boy was a deliberate target, not an accidental one. Putting a rock under the boy's head is a message. Was that widely known in the valley we're in?"

"Now that you ask, I suppose it was bar talk for a year or more. Range detectives getting paid when the rustler's head was on a rock. And someone put that rock under the boy's head. If one of the Miller boys had done this, there'd be no rock. The fact that there were no boot tracks, and no horse visible from down there, tells me the shooter was extra-careful, something young boys rarely are. Was the shooter Tom Horn or some other man? Maybe, but not likely. I've seen all I need to see. What say we head for the Bosler Station?"

CHAPTER 13

WHEN ANGUS ASKED Tommy who might know Tom Horn best, besides John Coble, the easy answer was Glendolene Kimmell.

"How'd she come to meet Horn?" Angus asked.

"Not sure, but the newspapers hounded her plenty. They say she was Horn's sweetheart."

"Was she?"

"Can't say. Horn spent some time with her. There was an attraction, on both sides. At least that's what folks around Bosler said. Whether it got to romance, nobody's sure. She was a nice-looking schoolteacher, with an education not many in Wyoming could match. Tom Horn's a rugged, handsome figure of a man, so it could be true. I never saw 'em together, but that doesn't count for much. A cowboy from the Miller ranch was talking his damn fool head off in Laramie one Saturday night. I was there. He said Tom Horn spent two days spooning her at the Miller ranch the week before Willie Nickell was shot."

"Is she a local girl from a ranching family?"

"No, I think she's from Missouri. Not much bigger than the ten-year old girls she taught in the Miller schoolhouse— one newspaper scribbler said she was but four and one-half feet tall. Another reporter, I think his name was Barlow, said Horn had a gentle dalliance with the schoolmarm. As I recall it, he even quoted Tom Horn about her—said Horn told Joe LeFors, "She was sure smooth people.""

"Smooth people? What's that mean?"

"Can't say. Not my way of talking. Now that we're talking about it, I remember another paper, the one I read at the café next to Bosler Station, described her as a 'petite vivacious piece of femininity.'"

"Really? I have to say, Tommy, your newspaper hounds up here use words like we use songs down in New Mexico—short, pretty, and always trouble."

"Well, we don't get many murder cases around here, and when one comes along where the victim is a school-boy, the defendant a hired gun, and there's a witness who gets whistled at everywhere she goes, it's like bees swarming in and out of a hive—only in this case it was a court house. You knew Miss Kimmell was called to testify in the coroner's inquest, didn't you?"

"Suppose so, but I didn't pay any mind to it," Angus said.

"Well, the busy bee reporters sure did. They even wrote about the day when Miss Kimmell came to Cheyenne on the train and was met at the depot by Tom Horn himself. Later, maybe at the courthouse, Horn gave one of his dumb interviews and was asked about walking her from the depot. He described her as a linguist, said she spoke half a dozen languages. He said she was half-Korean, one-quarter Japanese, and the rest German. But the reporter misspelled it as 'Corean.' Worst of all, Horn told the reporters she had become 'infatuated with him' after they met at the Miller ranch."

"Was she?"

"No, I think she was from Missouri—not some foreign country."

"I meant was she infatuated with him."

"Hell, I don't know. We don't use words like infatuated in Wyoming. He wasn't courting her; I can say that for sure. We have rules here about courting, coming to call, and such things as that. She was here as a single woman teaching in a small country school. Up here marriage is considered a woman's natural destiny. Otherwise, she's headed for the shame of spinsterhood. I can still remember my own mother getting after my sisters on that subject."

Angus thought a minute about asking about Tommy's own experience with sparking or keeping company with women, but thought better of it.

"So if it wasn't courting on the part of either Tom Horn or the school teacher, what was it? Infatuation?"

Tommy ignored his new friend.

"Tom Horn should have been nervous about her testimony. She knew a lot about the goings on at the Miller ranch school where both Miller boys and the Nickell kids were students. And because she had a natural way of talking, used educated words, and was well informed on history and science, everyone took her as real smart. Maybe too smart for a man who made his living with a gun. Anyhow, she was a witness at the inquest that the jurors took close notice of. I remember the exact date she testified at the coroner's inquest. It was July 23, 1901, and she was the first witness called that day. She . . ."

"Tommy, that strikes me interesting. How come you remember the exact date she took the stand. Were you sweet on her too?"

Tommy's face took on a hard stare. "No. I damn sure was not. Too short for my tastes. I remember the date because it was my birthday. I had celebration plans that day, but instead I spent the morning listening to Walter Stoll shoot questions at witnessnesses like a Gatling gun. That man can talk faster than most witnesses can listen, but Miss Kimmell was a match for him. You see, up until she took the stand, all the witnesses had been small-town Wyoming people. They take their time parsing answers. But not the schoolteacher. Well-spoken and certain of what she knew. She'd only been at the school two weeks and was just starting to know the Iron Mountain–area people. She was one of the first people to know about the murder."

"How'd that happen?"

"Strange and interesting; that's how. At nine-thirty in the morning, the day after they found Willie Nickell, Kels marched into her schoolroom and asked her to dismiss the children. He wanted to interrogate her—that's the word she said he used: interrogate. He insisted she tell him who was at the Miller house at the time his boy was killed. She was not straight up with him. She told the jurors she was very uncomfortable talking about the family's whereabouts. They had given her the teaching job and let her board at their house. She had breakfast with the family every morning—that's the time Kels was asking about."

"But she was willing to tell the coroner's jury about it, right?"

"She told them that when Kels accosted her, she was not sure her whether or not she had breakfast at the big table that morning. She was sure Jim and the two older sons were in the house. She would have noticed their absence, she said. She said Kels didn't give her time to think."

"Had Kels already told his side of it?"

"Well, I wasn't there when he testified a day or two earlier, but a deputy told me Kels had let it be known he thought the school teacher might be covering up for the Miller boys. Anyhow, back to her testimony. She wasn't sure when Kels barged into the school, but she was sure in court. She remembered 'with the utmost distinctness.' Mr. Miller, Gus, and Victor were all at home the day before Kels confronted her. They were all there, eating breakfast like any other day. Hell, Angus, she even remembered having a dish of strawberries that Thursday morning. Victor had picked them for her the previous morning. And that wasn't all."

Angus nodded. "She probably had good memory of other things that happened the day before the boy was killed, right?"

"You bet. She ended the school day about four the day before and walked across the field to the ranch house. Mr. Miller, a neighbor, and a woman named something-McDonald were there. I forget her first name—maybe she didn't say it. Anyhow, they had what she called an 'impromptu dance.' They were all happy and danced until around midnight. This was new to her, she said. It was a country dance, and everyone did it with great energy, she said. Mr. Miller and Gus and Victor were all dancing, happy, and cheerful. She confirmed for Mr.

Stoll that Victor had milked the cows the previous day, had breakfast with her and the rest of the family, and then went to Mr. Reed's house and from there to another neighbor's. Stoll asked her about meeting Tom Horn earlier in the week. She said he was a man with 'excellent features.' He rode a dark horse and his pronunciation was according to 'good English usage.'"

"Tommy, you could be a court stenographer yourself. You got a ken for remembering exact words people say."

"I wouldn't say that, Angus. I remember what people say, but never the exact words they use. There's a difference, you know."

"You bet," Angus said, mimicking two of Tommy's favorite words.

CHAPTER 14

LATE THAT MORNING, Tommy and Angus rode into the Stettler Shelter on the platform side of Bosler Station. The Stettler family had owned the big corral there as part of their ranch for over thirty years. Now it was owned by the railroad. They used it to hold stock; someone was running a boarding stable in the barn attached to the corrals. Tommy and Angus had split up four miles north of the Bosler Railroad Station— Tommy went to his ranch and told Angus to leave his horse at the boarding stable next door and he'd pick it up later. It was only twenty miles to Laramie, and Angus assured him the train would stop there mid-afternoon. He could buy a ticket to Laramie for a dollar fifty.

Angus assumed that the Bosler Station would be the anchor for a small Wyoming town. When he got there, he saw there was no real town. The railway station, complete with a short boardwalk and a sizeable stable next door—that's all there was.

No stores, houses, shops, or even a saloon. He dismounted and told the stable hand the horse belonged to Tommy George.

"She does, don't she though," the stable hand said, taking the reins. "Tack too. I'll oil the saddle the way Tommy likes it and give this sweet mare a block of fine alfalfa hay. Tommy will come by when it suits him and pony her mare back to his place. Unless you're buying her . . . are you?"

"No," Angus said, "I'm a friend of Tommy's. What's your name, son?"

"Hatcher."

"All, right Hatcher. Here's two dollars. Rub her down and give an extra nosebag of sweet grain. I just rode her for a couple days with Tommy appreciatin' Wyoming's meadow grass and ample water."

He took a seat on the bench outside the station house and sure enough, he heard the steam whistle about two-thirty. The clicktey-clack ride south to Laramie took less than an hour. From the Union Pacific station there, he walked three blocks up to the Kilmer Hotel and booked a room. As he walked, he couldn't help thinking how different Wyoming towns were from his home in Chama, New Mexico.

The next morning he went downstairs for breakfast and then took a walk up to the University of Wyoming campus and spent the morning in the college library. He got back to the hotel for a late lunch at almost two o'clock. The dining room was on the far side of the lobby. As he walked by the front desk, Laramie's daily newspaper—*The Daily Boomerang*—was on sale for a nickel. BOSLER RANCHER TOMMY GEORGE AMBUSHED AT HIS FRONT GATE.

The article was a scant three sentences. "Shortly after noon yesterday Laramie County Sheriff Duggal Dunipace reported another treacherous ambush in Bosler. A neighbor had reported by telegram from the Bosler Station to the Union Pacific Station in Laramie that Mr. Thomas George, a Bosler rancher, was killed by a person or persons unknown near the front gate of his property. No one is in custody, the Sheriff's office said. An investigation is in process."

Angus slammed hard on the desk bell and kept clanging it until the desk clerk came running from the side door to the kitchen. "Yes sir, what is the matter?" he stammered as he tried to reach the desk.

Angus faced the young clerk whose first effort at growing a moustache looked like a black twig barely gracing his upper lip. "You've a phone here. I need it to make a call to the U.S. Marshals office in Cheyenne."

"Well sir, I'm sure the head desk manager can accommodate you on that at four this afternoon when he comes on duty; there's a small charge for long distance, and . . ."

"Where's the damn phone?" Angus said.

"It's here, behind the desk on the shelf, but . . ."

Before he could finish the sentence, Angus vaulted over the desk, reached down, grabbed the phone, and fished his badge out of his vest pocket. "There will be no fee. Move far enough away so you can't hear."

He lifted the phone from the cradle and jammed the black touch bar until the operator came on line.

"Get me the U.S. Marshals office in Cheyenne, please. This is a government call and an emergency. Do it right now."

"Yes, Marshal, who do you wish to speak to there?"

"Put Deputy Marshal Joe LeFors on the line."

It took two more curt explanations to a different telephone operator and another clerk before Deputy U.S. Marshal Joe LeFors got on the line.

"Angus, they tell me you're damned excited about something but won't tell the clerk here what's got your dander up. How can I help you?"

"You can tell me everything you know so far about the ambush of Tommy George at the gate to his ranch yesterday up in Bosler. To say I'm excited ain't the half of it. I spent the better part of the last four days with Tommy and left him just a few hours before some bastard blew him out of the saddle at his front gate. I'll be riding up there myself as soon as I can, once you tell me what you know."

"All right now, Angus. Settle down. I need to know a lot more about your ride with him. You need to come in here to my office first. You have no jurisdiction up there. And besides . . ."

"Goddamn it, Deputy La Fors, if you can't tell me what happened, I'll dig it out of the Laramie Sheriff's office, but I'm guessing the ambush is somehow tied to the Tom Horn case. That's why I'm calling you first."

"I'll be happy to bring you up to date on the investigation soon, but now that I find you are a possible witness, we need to interview you in my office. Are you here or up at Bosler Station?"

"I'm in Laramie and headed to Bosler. Just answer me this. Have you got a suspect for the killing? Was Tommy shot with a 30.30? And did he die with a rock under his head? You can fill in the rest when I get down to Cheyenne, in a few days."

"No sir, no sir! That's not how this is going to work . . ."

Deputy La Fors realized he was talking to a dead line before he heard the buzzing sound.

"Sum bitch," he said to his assistant. "Find out when the next train is to Laramie, and get the sheriff up there on the line, right Goddamn now. I might have to arrest a deputy U.S. marshal, and I expect he will be a handful."

Angus went back up to his room, unpacked his Winchester model 1894 from the tarp around his bed roll, strapped on his Colt, and stuck his badge on the outside of his vest. After packing a box of .30-40 cartridges, his duster, and a hip bottle of brandy, he filled his water bag with the pitcher on the nightstand. He put everything in his saddlebags, including a notebook and a well-oiled map of Wyoming he'd bought at the hardware & tack store. Then, he dog-trotted back down to the Union Pacific and asked when the next train would head north to the Bosler Station.

"Tomorrow morning at 10:10. It's on the schedule there."

"Won't do. Where's the nearest boarding stable I can rent a horse?"

"That would be another block and a half across the tracks. Just take Ninth Street. You'll see it the other side of Wyoming Feed & Seed."

It took another thirty minutes to walk to the stable and pick a gray gelding that looked to be a long trotter. He told the stable hand not to bother with the tack and grabbed a saddle blanket, well-used saddle, and a seven-foot long set of reins spun out of a halter and bit. He swung the saddle up over the blanket, cinched it up tight, and eased the spur bit into the gray's mouth. He buckled the headstall and settled the reins. Then he attached the breast collar strap and loosened the rear cinch a notch.

He strapped on his spurs, tied his gear down behind the cantle, and told the wide-eyed stable hand he'd bring the gray back in a day or two as soon as he arrested an ambushing no-account bastard. As he mounted, he said, "Send an invoice by wire to U.S. Marshal George Ramsey in Denver. They will pay the fee—call it a week—the bastard I'm tracking might take that long."

Once horseback, he touched the gray lightly with one spur and moved him into a long trot. He alternated between an easy lope and a long trot for fifty minutes until he reached the Stettler Shelter barn at the Bosler Station. Hatcher was busy unloading hay from a big wagon. Two cowboys were sitting on the front bench, chewin' and spittin'.

"Hatcher, get me that dun mare I left with you yesterday and take this gray in your barn. He's sweated up some on the long trot from Laramie. I'll saddle the dun. You take the tack off this horse and store it till I get back."

"Yes sir, Deputy. I see the badge on your vest. I shoulda known it yesterday."

"You know about my friend, Tommy George?" Angus asked.

"Hell yes. Everybody knows. Those two cowhands are talking about it right now."

Angus took a few steps in their direction and asked, "Boys, I'm in a hurry here. I'd appreciate learning whatever you know about the ambush of my friend Tommy George."

They got up from the bench and came to him. The tallest one, with a hard set to his jaw, said, "Who are you, if you don't mind my asking?"

Angus flipped back the upper flap of his duster and pointed to his badge. "Name's Angus. You can call me Marshal. I'd be much obliged to hear whatever you know—all I know is what the headline said down in Laramie this morning."

"Hell, Marshal, we don't know much more. We're here waiting for the train to go down to Laramie. We ride for the Double Nine. Neither of us knew Mr. George, but we heard plenty about him on different ranches around here. He knew his horses and everybody who owned a spread knew him. There's no newspaper up here, so you probably know more 'n we do, except we know he was kilt yesterday."

Angus tightened the cinch on the mare and moved his rifle from the bedroll tarp to a scabbard on the offside of the saddle. He swirled the chamber of his Colt and stuck it back in his belt holster, grabbed a handful of mane with his left hand, and swung his right leg over the saddle.

"Holy shit," Hatcher said to the two cowboys. "That's a buckaroo you'd best not mess with."

The big difference between Angus's home territory in New Mexico and this part of southern Wyoming was the grass. Exhausting stretches of wide meadows riddled with small streams feeding grasses and stemmed flowers of all kind and manner. But New Mexico had a beautiful and intransigent countryside. Both had inexhaustible sky over rocky ground sometimes and nibble grass in others. Both were among the least-populated sections of the country at the turn of the twentieth century. In New Mexico they called it *el despoblado*, the uninhabited place. Up here, they called it Wyoming. Both had their troubles—long-range shooters firing from ambush and escaping within minutes of bodies hitting the ground.

As he fell into the mare's rhythm, he leaned into and out of the lope thinking about what little he knew at a personal level about Tommy George. He lived alone, after his wife left him for a banker in Wichita Falls, Kansas, her home ground. It was a farmer's town, not a ranching town, Tommy had said. His wife, whose name he didn't utter, went there twice to tend to her ailing mother. The second time she didn't come back. Seems she found a banker who came home every night not smelling like a horse. His nineteen-year old son was with his mother and the banker now. The banker paid his college tuition at Kansas State. More than Tommy could afford. That's all he was of a mind to say and Angus minded his manners.

Angus loped the first two miles northeast until he spotted the North Chugwater Creek. He knew Tommy's eighty acres were bounded by the creek on this side and mostly the Laramie River on the far side. There was a well-traveled wagon road that gave access to several dozen working ranches for the next fifty or sixty miles. The first few miles swung out in a semi-circle to his left, then narrowed for a half mile up a steep jagged hill. There was a wide saddle he could see in the distance with cedar and brush on both sides. The wagon road doubled back on itself another four or five miles northeast and crossed a creek without a name. The road formed a letter S, with wide curves.

In just under an hour he reached the fence line gate with the hand-lettered sign in black letters. *Thomas E. George—Horses,*

Hay, & Tack. Before getting any closer to the gate, Angus dismounted and ground tied the mare. He walked back a quarter mile looking down on the road for sign. He found three or maybe four horse tracks going toward the not-yet visible ranch house but only two tracks coming out from the gate. He squatted down to get a close look at the tracks coming out. They were about as fresh as the double sets headed into the ranch proper. The out-coming marks were deeper down into the soft sand. And one set was deeper than the other. A bigger horse, he thought. Maybe with a bigger man. Not Tommy, he was sure. Tommy was probably still on the inside of the fence—there were no wagon tracks. They'd want a wagon to haul his body to Laramie for autopsy. He was killed in ambush. The law demanded an inquest by a coroner's jury; that would come soon, Angus thought.

From this vantage point, the gate was about forty yards up the slope. He walked it leading the little mare—she knew she was near home. The fence gate was properly shut, so the last man out took the time to close the gate. Maybe both riders coming out closed the gate. It was the first one out he wanted, not the second. The second was whoever called the local deputy, who called Laramie. From there, the newspaperman got the story he'd read just a few hours ago. He walked both tracks slowly up and back. The deeper track also showed a longer stride—this one was at full gallop. The first one, maybe at a trot or an easy canter. He fixed the look of the deeper track as best he could in his mind.

Angus studied the sky above and around Tommy's ranch. He could detect no difference from yesterday's look and feel ten miles down at Bosler Station. The ground was settled and there was no sign of multiple horses or any wagons in or out of the gate. At least that's the way it looked from this far away. As he neared the gate, the mare got up on her toes, neighing and twisting a little. So, he mounted up. She was a little anxious. Horses always get that way when the barn is close by—this was home ground to her. She expected to walk through the gate and trot to whatever barns or corrals were on the other side of the hill. So he did. He turned her sideways along the gate and reached down for the looped wire that kept the gate shut. He opened the gate without letting go, sashayed her in, and closed the gate from the inside. Then he dismounted and tied her to a fence post ten feet down from the gate toward the ranch house.

On the inside of the fence, he could make out at least four tracks. One was an unmounted small horse. No rider. As he looked more carefully, he realized he was not looking at a horse track, but at a burro track, unshod and not mounted. Then, as though he and the dun mare were being watched, he heard the familiar bray of a mature burro. The bray was quickly met by a neigh from the dun. She knew that burro. It probably had the run of the property and was never penned in except for vetting. They nuzzled one another. The burro paid him no mind, acting like he was not even there. But he knew the burro was witness to whatever happened around this gate yesterday afternoon. A burro had watched the ambush.

He walked close to the fence line down the gentle slope toward the house and got his first look at the ground twenty yards away, down slope. Hoof prints suggesting a horse bucking or twirling and a pool of dried blood. Boot prints and other horse marks around the blood. Wagon ruts in the road from there toward the ranch house. Goddamn, Angus thought. Tommy was hit here, probably in the back. It might have blown him out of the saddle. His body is probably still at the house, with whoever took it there yesterday. The bastard's not only an ambusher; he's a back shooter.

As he stood still looking in all four directions from the inside of the gate, he noticed another hoof track just a few feet inside the upper fence line headed up the ten-degree slope away from the ranch house, which he still could not see. He walked back past the gate and followed the single track upslope. It looked to be the bigger horse track he'd spotted outside the fence—deep into the sandy shale—a mounted horse. But maybe not.

He figured the shot came from above, to the right of the gate as you came in. More cover up there to lay low and keep your horse out of sight. He stopped and went back to the gate and unsheathed his Winchester from the scabbard. Then he took the coiled rope from the mare's saddle horn. Easing his way over to the burro, who was still nosing the mare, he looped the rope around the burro's neck. He didn't like it and turned to give him the kick he had coming.

"Easy there, Señor Burro, I mean you no harm. Just let me lead you a little."

He double looped the mare's reins to the fence post so she wouldn't follow them and spoil the tracks. Then he walked the burro up along the inside of the fence and away from the ranch house. The burro resisted but fell in place until they reached a small flat place about a hundred feet up, along the inside of the fence. All of a sudden the hoof tracks made a sharp left turn toward a stand of acorn and thick little aspen trees, forty feet inside the fence line. The burro stopped and brayed the way an irritated burro does when forced to do something he doesn't want to do. Angus stopped and tied the burro to the closest fence pole.

From there he followed the track slowly into the ranch proper. It was lightly forested with cedar, oak brush, and acorn trees. Must be steady rain up here, he mused to himself. There were scattered boulders ranging from one to three feet above ground. As he walked slowly, looking down at the ground rather than ahead, he followed the track for about fifty feet right into the aspen stand. That's where he got the first real sense he was on the right track. The ground was mushed with both horse and boot tracks. The bastard had dismounted here and led his horse into the aspen stand where it would not be seen from the gate. He walked into the thick mix of aspen and tall brush.

Twenty feet in, he found solid evidence. Fresh horse dung. Fresh boot tracks, made deep into the side of the hill. Broken shrub branches and several chewed weeds where the horse had been tied to a thick aspen. He followed the boot track on into the stand and out again after another ten feet. The little clearing was behind a rock mound about two feet tall. He found that the soft sandy ground was mushed out to reveal the shape of a man. The bastard took his shot from here, he thought. On his belly. The boot marks five or six feet behind the rock were toe marks, not heels.

Got you, you bastard, Angus thought. Here's where you laid down to make your ambush work. You used this rock as a rifle mount. That groove sliced in the rock made this a fine shooting hide. Your time came when Tommy opened the gate to his ranch. Once he was inside, you lined him out. You're about seventy or eighty yards out with a clear daylight shot, and you got him. In the back. Now, I got you. And I'm coming for you.

He squatted behind the mounting rock for a few minutes thinking about how the kill shot was taken. It occurred to him he still might be missing something, so he stretched out on top of the mushed up ground. Propping himself on his elbows with his gut flat and his toes holding his boots up, he imagined what the gate area must have looked like when the bastard hit Tommy.

Was Tommy mounted or had he dismounted to latch the gate from the inside? No, Tommy wouldn't dismount just to open or close a gate. All his horses would have been trained to sashay sideways to get that job done. That meant the angle of the bastard's rifle to the ground up here would not have been exactly horizontal. He would have had to tilt the barrel, say about ten or fifteen degrees up. He lined the shot out by doing that.

As he laid there thinking about the shot, he wondered how well sound would carry from here down to the gate. He laid his gun barrel in the notch and assumed a shooting position with his left eye lined out over the rear and front sites. Then he eased back on the firing hammer. The telltale click was clear in his ear but he saw no movement from the mare tied to the gatepost. He used the lever to jack a 30.40 cartridge into his firing chamber. That damn sure got the mare's attention as she swiveled to look upslope at the rock he was behind.

All right, you bastard, so you jacked a shell before Tommy reached the gate. He gave the bastard the benefit of the doubt about not carrying a riffle in a scabbard, or while looking for a shooting spot with a shell in the chamber. Good way to shoot yourself in the foot, if you stumble.

So his man was careful. Maybe he'd shot at ambush before. What else, he thought? You picked the high ground for a gun-fight in case the target was just wounded and fired back, maybe with a revolver drawn from a belt holster. Tommy had one on yesterday. He most always wore his gun when horseback off his own ranch. Most men did.

Once he got a look at Tommy's body he'd know whether the bastard shot more 'n once, and that would tell whether he had to jack more shells into the chamber. More brass to pick up, and more time for the target to react. There was no brass around the rock, or twenty feet away where his horse was tied to a thick aspen. Now was the time to take a careful look at the ground down the slope in front of him.

Lifting the loop of the burro's neck, a nagging thought hit him. Why had the bastard walked his horse inside the gate in the first place? It locked him inside the ranch proper with no quick way out if the shooting didn't come out his way. Why didn't he take his shot from outside the fence—quicker and easier getaway, right? Nothing came to him about this mystery.

Once back downslope at the gate, he mounted the mare and shooed the burrow down toward the ranch house. There was lots of horse track once inside the fence, and he didn't take the time to match anything up with what he now knew was the kill site.

A half mile down the twisty road, he found Tommy's ranch house. It was near the same color as the ground around it and burrowed into another upward slope so deeply you could enter either its bottom or top floor at ground level. Angus had never seen another ranch house like this one. There were shuttered windows on both floors, two smoke stacks visible, and a wide porch on both sides of the front view. A hitching rail fronted the house on the right side, and a round brick well house took up the left side. Two outhouses were fanned downwind toward the barns. The doors of both faced the other way from the road. The barn was bigger by half and was attached to a half dozen mid-size corrals. There were at least twenty head of big-eyed horses staring at him as he approached from the downwind side.

If the horses were curious about him, the two figures sitting on armchairs on the porch were not. Both jumped up as though he was just the man they were looking for.

"Are you here to take the body?" one boy asked. He looked to be maybe twelve. They were obviously brothers, wearing matching denim trousers with dark work shirts not tucked in. Their boots were for riding not dancing, and both were wearing roweled spurs.

"No, I'm not," Angus said as he dismounted and looped a rein once around the hitching rail.

"I'm here to find out what happened—I'm a lawman and a friend of Tommy George. You boys here alone?"

"Yes sir," the other boy said. "Ma said we were to stick here until somebody in charge came to get him."

"By 'him,' I suppose you mean Tommy George, right?"

"Yes, sir," the other boy answered. "We live two ranches down, past the Cross S. Ma said she'd be back soon as she got things buttoned at our place—you know livestock chores are waiting for us. Can we go now?"

"Do either one of you know what happened here? I mean to Tommy George."

"We know he's killed and on the kitchen table, back there," he said, pointing to the near side of the bottom floor. The other boy clarified. "But he's wrapped up in a clean tarp. Ma cleaned his wounds and seen to the tarp. Can we go now?"

"Boys, that's up to your mother. Let's do this: one of you head on home and tell you mother I'm here. My name's Angus. I'm a deputy U.S. marshal from Colorado and a friend of Mr. George."

"We got to do things together, Mr. Marshal. Ma said."

"Fine. Both of you saddle up. I'll stay and guard the body in your absence. That's what you've been doing, right, guarding the body?"

"No sir, Ma didn't say nothing about guarding. She just said stay here till I get back. She went to the Millers because they have a phone. Only ranch close by that does."

Angus decided not to argue with the boys and went in the house to find Tommy's body. He didn't have to walk far. The front porch had two doors—one near the middle and one at the far side. The far side door was closed, the middle door open. Angus chose the far side, because that door was closed and because he could see a chimney-stack extending out from the side wall and willowing up over the second floor. Kitchen stove and closed door—that's where they took him.

He could smell it before the door swung wide. The long kitchen table had been cleared and an oversized ranch tarp laid on it. Tommy's body was wrapped tight from neck to toe and tied with rawhide strips. But they had not strapped it around his head—maybe because it was no longer really a head—more like a crushed Iowa pumpkin, yellowed and punctured, with most of the blood washed off.

The coroner would say later, "The deceased died from external and internal wounding of the head, face, and cranial vault as well as from partial severance of the spinal cord."

According to Doctor Arroyo, the Laramie County coroner, the shot blew Tommy off his horse, causing bruising and skin damage. Based on what the woman who found him said, Dr. Arroyo surmised he was shot while horseback, went off the horse on his left side, and died almost instantly. That bullet did not exit but was found at autopsy to be lodged in Tommy's right jawbone—through the back of his cranium, through brain tissue, through the frontal lobe, and lodged in his jaw.

The woman who found Tommy dead on his ranch road came in an hour after her boys had been shooed home by Angus. She found Angus sitting across the room, with his Winchester across his knees, looking like he'd been ghost sitting.

"I'm Mrs. Bruce," she said. "My boys told me you were in here and you're a lawman. Can't say I've seen you, and our family has been in this area for nigh on twenty-five years."

Angus got up slowly and leaned his rifle against the wall. He pulled a blue bandanna from his rear pocket, said, "excuse me," and blew his nose. He walked to the sink, found a tin cup, and poured some water from a half-gallon Wesson jar on the counter. Taking a long pull and breathing in slowly, he faced the woman.

"I am sorry to trouble you, Ma'am. Your boys were courteous and curious. Would you mind sitting with me on the porch? I have questions."

He learned her first name was Etta, her husband was Ivan Bruce, and they ran a small cow-calf operation two ranches down. Like all the other ranchers, they knew Tommy George as kind, and as reliable a neighbor as anyone could have—she called him a man you could count on, no matter what.

"How'd you know he was down?" Angus asked.

"My boys saw him on the ground late yesterday morning. They were on the other side of the fence headed to the Cross S to pick up a colt we had turned out there. Well, actually they were on the way back when they heard a shot close by. We all knew Mr. George was away for a few days. We look after his place when he's away, selling or training horses."

"He was with me, for the last three days. I left him at Bosler Station yesterday morning. Can you tell me when they heard a gunshot and where they were at that time?"

"Well, sir, I can . . ."

"Please call me Angus."

"Angus what, if you don't mind my asking?"

"It's just Angus."

"Fine by me," she said. "Now the boys said they heard the shot when they crested the upper hill, and the dry creek. We call it the no-creek because it's just run off, not ground water. It's about a mile from Mr. George's front gate. It came from that direction, so the boys galloped the last mile and a half."

"What's the first sign of trouble they told you about?"

"They saw a man on the ground and a loose horse pawing the ground about halfway to the curve in the road before you get to the ranch house here. So, they rode on the outside of the fence and saw was Mr. George on the ground in a bad way. And they could see he wasn't moving, and . . ."

"Excuse me, Ma'am, was the gate open or closed?"

"I didn't ask, but I know now it was closed."

"How so?"

"Because my husband asked them last night at supper after he got back to the house from his hay-baling job over at the Wintershed place. It was after dark by then. But he came over here this morning, and . . ."

"Excuse me again, but did your boys see anyone when they were riding full out on the way here when they heard a gunshot?"

"Not that they said any such thing to me. You see, they didn't know he was shot. So they weren't looking for anything like that. When they heard the shot, it didn't mean anything. This is Wyoming. But they were on the road just a mile or two from Mr. George's gate. It didn't spook them, they are only twelve, but you know, this is Wyoming."

"When did they learn he was shot?"

"Well now that you mention it, I was the one who told them, this morning. They thought he got thrown and broke his neck and bashed in his skull."

"Didn't they see a bullet wound on his shoulder and blood on his chest?"

"No, they didn't. They could see he was either unconscious or dead. At their age they would not know the difference. He wasn't moving. So they rode home lickety-split. Our gate is just two miles north."

"Hmm," Angus said. "Seems like one of them would have stayed with him if they didn't know his condition while the other rode for help."

"No, Mr. Angus. That's not our way. The boys do things together. They are twins, you know, not the exact identical kind, the other kind. But they have not been apart for any reason ever."

"Yes, Ma'am, sorry to have upset you. They seem like good boys to me."

"No offense taken. Now where were we?"

"You were about to tell me what you saw when they came home and fetched you here."

"Yes, it took a little while because I had to put the horses in their traces on our small ranch wagon—the one we use to go to town for supplies. Somehow I had the presence of mind to know we'd need a wagon to help Mr. George, whether he was alive or not. I put some medical necessaries in the box, just in case. It was probably an hour before I got here."

"Any idea how long it took the boys to ride from here to their home once they saw Tommy down inside his fence line?"

"They rode hard. So maybe twenty-five or thirty minutes. And yes, and I can see your next question. No, I did not see anything on the way here. The boys were riding alongside, and they didn't see anything either."

"Yes, Ma'am."

"When I got here, I felt for a pulse, put my ear on his chest, and knew he was dead. Unlike the boys, I could see . . . I hate to say it, the carnage at the back of his skull was the most frightful thing I've ever seen. I thought it was a shotgun blast because his skin was all torn up and the blood had clotted and dried on his neck."

"Your boys would know how different a shotgun sounds from a rifle, wouldn't they?"

"Sure, they go turkey hunting with Ivan, their father, and deer hunting too. You don't take a shotgun to hit deer. They could tell that. They heard a gunshot from a rifle, or maybe a pistol. Not a shotgun."

It took another half-hour but Angus learned she had sent the boys home after they moved the body from the road onto the kitchen table. Then she drove her wagon to the Miller school house and used the phone there to call Laramie. Late last night, two deputies came to this house, inspected the body, and then rode to the Bruce ranch and talked to her and her boys.

She left an hour later when Deputy Sheriff DeFrances and Dr. Arroyo rode up to the house and found Angus sitting on the same chair Mrs. Bruce had left him in.

CHAPTER 15

THE TWO MEN DISMOUNTED and tied their horses to the rail closest to the kitchen. Angus heard them but didn't get up. He knew they were here to take Tommy's body back to Laramie where they'd autopsy and embalm him.

Dr. Arroyo spoke first. "I'm sorry, sir, but I'm here to take Mr. George's body back to Laramie. He had no family, so the duty falls on the county. Could I ask your full name, sir?"

"You could, but my name's Angus and here's my badge," he said, flipping open his duster to display his badge."

Deputy Sheriff De Frances walked to Angus with his hand outstretched. "Marshal, I'm Deputy Sheriff DeFrances. Just before we left Laramie, I talked to U.S. Deputy Marshal LeFors on the telephone, and he told me I was to bring you back to Laramie right fast. He said something about jurisdictional preference."

"Let me make it easy for you, Deputy DeFrances. Are you arresting me?"

"No sir, no one said anything like that to me."

"Then, I'm not going back with you to Laramie. I'll be back there in a day or two. I've got work to do here. You tell LeFors I'm considering connections between the Tom Horn case and the ambush of my friend Tommy George. And your boss, the county sheriff, has no trouble with my help on this case, does he? I'm the last man to see him alive, and the first man to scout this place for evidence. If you want to help me, well, that'd be mighty fine."

"Well, to tell you the truth, Marshal, I do not know what the sheriff wants. It seems to me that the deputy U.S. marshal in Cheyenne is leading the Tom Horn case. If this one is connected to that one, don't you think you ought to go back with us and talk to Joe LeFors? You know he carries a lot of weight up here, don't you?"

"I do not know what he carries, other than securing confessions from unsuspecting suspects. And I'll talk to him in person, up here, or by phone when I get close to one. Meanwhile, I am tired and need some sleep. I'll camp across the Laramie River on the east side. Do you boys need any help lifting the body into your wagon?"

Angus took the little mare to the horse trough and let him suck up a bellyful. He went into the barn and borrowed two gunnysacks of sweet grain and a nosebag. Then he mounted up and headed east for the far side of Tommy George's forty acres. He knew the Laramie River crisscrossed the property line about three miles from the ranch house. It took less than an hour in the failing light.

Just before the light disappeared, he spotted the eastern fence line. He hoped to find a loose fence post he could lie down and cross over. Or maybe there would be a cattle gate close by. When he got closer, he saw the gate and smiled. Tommy, my friend, I should have known you'd have your property properly fenced and gated, he said to himself. He rode up to the gate, unlatched it, and sashayed the mare across the smooth wagon road. On the other side he closed and latched the gate, turning to cross the Laramie River.

He was half way across when he looked upstream and saw Marguerite Esme's big wagon parked and her mules tied to a hitching line. There was a small campfire burning, but he couldn't see any movement. So he nudged the little mare with a tap of his right spur and stepped down into the river and into the flow. The depth was between two and three feet, so they managed it quick and easy.

He loped up the bank and through some heavy brush to a clearing on the east side of the river. He reined in the mare, leaned back in the saddle, and pondered his dilemma. Remembering what Tommy had said about not approaching Marguerite sideways, he was unsure what to do now. Should he dismount and lead the mare the fifty yards that now separated them from those mules? Hadn't they picked up his horse's scent yet? He decided to sit in the saddle and wait it out. It didn't take long.

"Angus," a female voice cried out in the dim light. "I been watching you from my wagon seat for the last two miles. You're still riding Tommy's horse. I've been waiting for you."

Angus walked his horse up and stopped about thirty feet from the little campfire. To his surprise, he saw her sitting five feet off the ground on the wagon seat with a pair of army binoculars strung from a leather strap around her neck. And she had a shotgun splayed across her lap. As he moved closer, she took the binoculars off and stuck the shotgun in a short scabbard on the side of the wagon seat.

"Monsieur Angus, I've been waiting for you. We have sad things to talk about."

Angus tied the mare to a large juniper tree and walked closer to the fire.

"Miss Marguerite, you are a surprise to beat all. When I saw you sitting up high on the wagon with a shotgun close by, I worried for a minute that maybe you were waiting for me."

"You were right to worry, but you have nothing to fear from my shotgun. I have been waiting here for two days. I knew someone would come the back way from Tommy George's ranch house. I'm glad it was you. *Je suis en deuil.*"

"I don't speak foreign languages, Miss. What are you saying?"

"I am in mourning. You are too."

During the next hour, Angus learned things about Tommy and this young girl that astounded him. Marguerite dodged around, as was her way, by telling him part of her life story before she'd talk about Tommy.

"Do you know, Monsieur Angus, about the Northwest Mounted Police up in Canada? No, I didn't think you would. It is the only police north of the Canadian border. I ask you that because it is part of a sad story I must tell you if you are now investigating the shooting of Tommy George. That is right, *s'il vous plait*? You are tracking the killer of your friend, right?"

"You bet. What do you know about it?"

"I will tell you, but first you must know about my half-brother. His name is Jean Louis. He was born in British Columbia to my father and his first wife. She died, and my father, who was working with the Hudson Bay Company, was alone and miserable. Only when he found my mother in Montana did he find a reason to stay living. I don't know what caused it, but his son, my half-brother Jean Louis, became estranged. He is maybe ten years older than me. My father only talked to me about him one time. He said I had a half-brother. That was just two years ago. And then . . ."

"Don't mean to interrupt, Miss, but what does your brother have to do with the ambush of Tommy George?"

"Jean Louis is my half-brother. I'm afraid he shot Tommy, oh God . . ."

She didn't cry; she shook and wailed at the sky—opening and closing her eyes, wrapping her arms around her chest, and rocking back and forth as though a thunderbolt had struck her. She'd been sitting on a small three-legged stool like farriers use, and she just fell off to the side as it slid out from under her. Angus jumped up and helped her to her feet. He wrapped one arm around her to steady her, but she just went rigid like she'd turned into stone.

He moved her by sort of shuffling his feet back to the big wagon wheel and eased her down onto the ground with her back to the spokes. She stared at the ground as though she couldn't stand the sight of him.

"You just sit there a minute, Miss. I've got something in my saddle bag that might be of some comfort."

He went to his horse, dug in the offside saddlebag, and found the pint bottle of brandy. Unscrewing the cap, he said,

"Just you take a small swig of this; it'll settle your nerves some. Don't try to talk. I'll get some more wood on your fire."

There was no shortage of downed limbs and dead branches around, so he built the fire up, took a pull on the pint bottle himself, and waited for Marguerite to steady herself. She never moved her head to keep him in view. He walked Tommy's mare to the hitching line, tying her twenty feet away from the mules. He pulled off his saddle, saddle blanket, bags, and bedroll tarp and hung his bridle, headstall, and rope on a tree branch. Dragging a dead four-foot-long pine log, he set himself a place for his saddle and gear on the far side of the fire. The coffee from the pot on the metal grill next to the fire was lukewarm, but it was OK with a slurp of brandy in it. He guessed it was ten or fifteen minutes before she broke her stare at nothing and turned her head in his direction.

"Mister Angus," she mumbled, making a sign of some kind with her right hand, "I must tell you about Jean Louis first, and then you can ask me about how I know Tommy George."

"I got time," Angus answered, crossing his outstretched legs so his spur rowels were not propping up his boots.

It was more family history than Angus wanted to know. "Jean Louis was trouble for my dad and his first wife. When Jean Louis was a little boy he stole fruit from a neighboring orchard, hard candy from the Hudson's Bay store, and kisses from unwilling girls at the Christian school. When he was fifteen, he became a stable hand for the Northwest Mounted Police in Calgary. He was good with horses and kept care of their new stock, including riding the new ones to get them ready for mounted patrol. I'm not sure, but maybe he took care of their horses to get a bunk in the barn and a seat at the big eating table. He might have worked for them for two years. I don't remember what he said."

"So he had a hard life. What's that got do with killing Tommy?"

"I'm telling you, Monsieur, but I only know one way. They let him ride one of their horses like it was his own. They gave him a saddle, and he could go anywhere when he wasn't taking care of the other horses. One night he stole that horse, and another one. He ran away from Calgary to a town I think was in Montana. He sold the other horse there and went to a saloon that had some young girls and paid them for you-know-what, don't you? Then the Sheriff there put him in put him in jail. They had a wanted poster on him from the Mounted Police in Calgary."

"Miss, you know you're trying my patience, don't you?"

"Well, how can I tell you what he did if you don't know who he was?"

Angus took another pull on the brandy bottle.

"So then the Mounted Police came and arrested him and took him back to Canada. He was Canadian. A judge put him in a prison for five years, but they let him out in only two years."

"Why?" Angus asked.

"Because of what happened to him in that prison."

Angus felt no sympathy for this boy, but knew he had to listen or she would shudder and wail again.

"Miss, I am sorry about him, but you said you were afraid he shot Tommy. Now, let's talk about that. Can we do that? Why would he want to shoot Tommy?"

She moved her head in circles and rubbed both ears with her hands. Then with her shoulders curling forward, she mumbled the story out, a few words at a time.

"Because of me. That's why. You know, because I don't hide my life. I like men. I like to bed them, and I like screwing. I did it with Tom Horn. I did it with Tommy too. But with Tommy, it was different. He said he loved me, and I think he did, in his way. I am only twenty-six. He was over forty. His first wife left him, and it cut him to the quick. He only came to me for comfort, and I took him to bed, in my wagon. And Jean Louis learned that from me."

"Why would that make your brother want to kill him?"

"Because of what the prison did to Jean Louis. He went to prison when he was just sixteen and some older men there did bad things to him. I don't know what, but he was never the same. He hated them and anyone that forced sex."

"Forced sex? That's what you're saying? What in god's name did that have to do with Tommy? He never forced you, right? You were willing, right? What 'n hell are you talking about?"

Angus was standing now, leaning forward toward Marguerite, feeling a tingle in his chest and cold in his fingers. She said nothing.

"Goddamn it to hell and back, woman. You are confounding me."

"I told Jean Louis that I didn't want to have sex with Tommy George. I only did it because I felt sorry for him. Then he blew up and hit me. He called me a whore and said I was just like those men in prison. He said Tommy was using me just like those men in prison used him. And he would get even for both of us."

"When did you tell him this?"

"Three days ago. Down along the Laramie River, just west of Laramie. He found me there when I was going to the county fair and selling some of my oils and tin work."

"So he told you three days ago he was going to kill Tommy? Is that what you're saying?"

"No, he never said anything like that. But I could see he was mad about Tommy and me at the same time. I was stupid, but I told him maybe I could talk to Tommy about giving him a job on the ranch since his own son was in Kansas now."

"So you brought him up here? On the open range side of his ranch?"

"*Qui,* but he was always blowing up at something and then forgetting it. He said maybe I was right, maybe if I asked, Tommy would give him a job and a place to live on his ranch."

"Why would Tommy do that?"

"You know Tommy. He was a horse breeder, trainer, and trader. Maybe Jean Louis could work for Tommy. So I drove my wagon up here since we always met here. Tommy always knew when someone was over here. His horses and his dog told him that. Jean Louis came with me, but as soon as I got my mules out of their traces, he jumped back on his horse and went across the river to Tommy's back gate. I told him about that too. I was so stupid!"

"How did you find out Tommy had been killed?"

"I didn't know for sure. This is the back gate. Jean Louis knew about this gate. This is public range over here, and no one hardly ever comes over this way, except to move cattle. This way he could ride into Tommy's ranch from here and come out and no one would see him on the road that goes down to Bosler."

"Now you listen to this question carefully. What exactly makes you think he killed Tommy? Don't you lie to me."

"I saw Jean Louis ride through that gate right over there. The one you just came through. It seemed like a lot of time passed. Then I heard a rifle shot. Jean Louis was a good shot and lived mostly off the game he killed. I just sat here and waited—too scared to go in there and too afraid of what I heard. Then, about an hour later, Jean Louis came out. Through that same gate you just came through. Come dawn, you can cross the Laramie River again. You'll see two fresh horse tracks. His and yours."

"You heard just one shot, or more?

"Just one, I think. Were there two?"

"When he came through, did your Goddamned brother tell you he shot Tommy?"

"No."

"But you're sure he did?"

"*Qui*. Jean Louis was not a strong man. Sometimes he acted just like a boy. I never saw him cry. But he was crying when he rode past me, like I wasn't even here. He looked through me, not at me. I screamed at him, but he paid no attention. He rode north, fast, and he didn't look back."

CHAPTER 16

I N THE FALSE DAWN that gives presence to the eastern sky,
Angus got up, brushed the mare, saddled and bridled her,
and walked her down to the edge of the Laramie River. He
could see the fence line stretching and the gate he'd come
through last night and somehow dreaded finding the proof
that Marguerite's crazy story was true. He'd looked over his
shoulder at her wagon but there was no movement, except for
the mules rustling a little. He laid his rein on the mare's neck
and clicked her down the bank and into the slow-moving
water. At the edge, she stopped to drink. He mumbled to the
horse and to the rising sun.

When he got across the river he stopped again about ten
yards outside the gate, dismounted, and ground tied the mare.
Then, as slow and careful as he could, he took short steps
looking for fresh horse tracks.

"Damnit to hell and back," he hollered at himself and
the rising sun. There they are, you old fool. Another horse

track you never saw. There's my track coming out and his— her Goddamned brother—just like she said. He followed the other track, and it veered off to the south a quarter mile from the gate. It turned south and up into a tree line, mostly scrub juniper, oak, and some Aspen stands.

It led him up behind the ranch house and the western gate everybody else used. Before he got there, he knew what he'd find. Jean Louis's horse tracks didn't go out that west gate like he thought. They came back on the upside of the ranch and crossed from west to east, crossing the Laramie River just like his Goddamned little sister said he had.

All right you sum bitch, he said to himself. You're on your way to Montana now. Maybe Canada. But I'll catch you, sum bitch. He spun the mare around and headed back to Tommy's ranch house. He wasn't surprised to find Etta Bruce and both her boys busy taking care of his horses, dogs, chickens, a milk cow, and two young calves he'd been raising for winter beef. He could see her wagon with two mules in harness. The boys were pitching hay from the barn into a wheelbarrow on the down side of the big fenced-in corrals.

"Ma'am," he said, as he dismounted and tied the mare to the hitching rail.

"Marshal," she replied, nodding in his direction. "Have you had anything to eat this morning? I am getting ready to fry some eggs for the boys and myself. We've been here a couple hours getting the house ready."

"Well, that would be mighty fine Mrs. Bruce," he answered. "I have a track on a man I have reason to believe shot Tommy. What do you mean you're getting the house ready? Ready for what?"

"Come on in the kitchen, and we'll trade. I can tell you what we're doing with the house and property, and you can tell us what kind of track you have on whoever shot Tommy senior."

Over coffee, eggs, bacon, and toasted bread, they surprised one another. He told them a little about the man he thought had shot Tommy. Etta told him what she and her husband thought would happen to the ranch, stock, and this house.

Etta said, "You know Tommy has a son, don't you?"

"Well yes, but I thought the boy and his mother left him and moved back to her home somewhere in Kansas years ago."

"It was years—going on seven now. She did not like ranch life, but their only child, Thomas Edward George, loved ranch life—he even liked our winters. He was fourteen when his mother took him to Kansas, so that makes him about twenty-one or twenty-two now. We heard he went to college. Anyhow, the medical examiner, Dr. Arroyo, found them and somehow managed to get them on the phone through a bank in Wichita. He talked to Tom's son too. Folks around here who knew family seven years ago called the boy Tom and his father Tommy. My boys were younger but played with Tom, the son, a little bit back then. I can tell you that Tom was absolutely the center of Tommy's life. Anyhow, Dr. Arroyo said that Tom George would be here later this week, via the Union Pacific Railroad to Cheyenne, and then on to here through Laramie. He thinks the boy is coming to stay, since he's Tommy's sole heir and this ranch now belongs to him."

Angus said, "I only knew Tommy for two weeks, but learning he has a son to take over his ranch sounds mighty fine to me."

"What can you tell us about the killing? Do you know the man you think ambushed Tommy?"

"No, I don't know him. But he has a sister you might have heard of; her name is Marguerite Esme. She has a big wagon and sells things out of it. Do you know her?"

"Most families know about her. It's not something we talk about. You know the saying, if you can't say something good about a person then . . . Well, you know the saying."

"I do. I'll mind the saying and say no more. But I am near certain her brother, Jean Louis, shot Tommy. His full name is Jean Louis Esme . He's a French Canadian but I think he lives mostly in Montana now. The motive is a bad feeling he had about Tommy and his little sister. I think he's on the run now, headed north to Montana. That's his home territory. I've got to go back down to Laramie City and talk to the sheriff there. I also need to talk to deputy U.S. Marshal Le Fors. Then, I'll make a plan to find the sum bitch Jean Louis. Pardon my language, Ma'am."

"No offense taken, Angus, this is Wyoming, you know. Men talk like that and apologize for it later."

"By any chance are you going down to Bosler Station when you finish up here, Ma'am?"

"I assume you want to leave Tommy's little roan here, right?"

"I do."

"Fine, the boys and I will take you, and they can get a candy stick at the stable store from Hatcher."

When Angus got to Laramie City, he told Sheriff Smalley everything he knew. Turns out, the sheriff knew a little about

Jean Louis. He'd never been arrested for anything, but he did frequent the dance halls and paid for time with nighttime women when he came to town. He was known as a skilled hunter, and a few ranchers had hired him to rid cougars and bears from the high ridges on the west side of the Laramie River. He was a crack shot and a mean drunk.

Angus caught the train the next day down to Cheyenne and made peace with Joe LeFors. To his surprise, Le Fors thought he should quit investigating Tom Horn and instead look into the murder of Tommy George. He told Angus he'd dig into their records and let him know what they found about Jean Louis Esme.

Three days later, after talking to Sheriff Smalley and his deputies, he learned that Jean Louis favored northwest Wyoming and guided hunting trips up between Casper and Jackson. He was known slightly in the Tetons and Yellowstone. Apparently, he had friends in the tribal areas around Jackson. They told him the best place to start would be Casper and then to work his way west if there was no track of him in Casper. On the fourth day after Tommy was killed, Angus caught the train north from Laramie to Casper.

CHAPTER 17

A NGUS DIDN'T KNOW MUCH about railroads except that he hated riding them—all closed in and rocking from side to side. Not at all like riding a long-legged horse looking up at a clear sky and enjoying the forward and backward swing on a fine-fitting saddle. But he knew he needed to travel more than a hundred miles at three times the speed of a horse if he was to get ahead of Jean Louis. The railroad was the only way he could do it. The agent at the Laramie Station told him the Union Pacific train up north to Casper was a 190-mile run. There was some slow going, but his train schedule said the run from Bosler Station to Casper would take nine hours, give or take, considering water stops and cows loose on the track.

"You're lucky," the man said. "There are two passenger cars on today's train. It will pull in here at 12:40 from Cheyenne and turn north to Bosler Station. There's a thirty-minute stop here for passenger comfort and to load whatever stock or logs will be heading to Casper—pretty big town, that Casper."

"OK, I'll buy a one-way ticket. I'll be there after dark tonight, right?"

"Yes, sir, too late for dinner, but I'm told there's dance halls up there open until way after dark, what with the dancin' and all."

Like always, Angus looked at things through the lens of how long the job would take. He festered about when he'd be back home in Chama with Jill. She did not deserve him gone for this long. Simple: just catch and jail that sum bitch Jean Louis and get home by Thanksgiving. Maybe he'd find his man around Casper. The local mortician could handle the body if Jean Louis resisted. If not, he'd let the sheriff in Casper handle getting the sum bitch back down to Laramie for trial.

Angus heard the train whistle a few minutes before the locomotive chugged to a stop at Laramie Station. The first men to get off the rear passenger car were a surprise. He owed Deputy Joe LeFors a return phone call but had planned to make it from Casper. He got off the bench and walked toward the men. Deputy LeFors gave him a shout and a grin. Both were a surprise.

"Well, I'll be damned if it ain't the roving marshal from Colorado himself waiting here to talk to me. Angus, you are a man that takes some tracking just to keep you in sight. How'd you know I was on this train? We got some serious confabbing to do, don't we?"

Angus didn't know whether to confront LeFors or wait him out.

"You might well be damned Joe Le Fors. When we last talked you were a mite upset with my investigating. So let's settle on this bench right here. I can give you twenty-nine minutes. Then I'm taking a train ride up to Casper—they tell me it's a lively place if you like drinking and dancing."

LeFors introduced the man with him. "Angus, shake hands with a man who is interested in the Horn case. This is Detective Marble from the Pinkerton Agency in Denver. He's also interested in the Tommy George case."

"Mr. Marble, I only met him, Tommy George, ten days ago, but I spent near a week with him looking into the Tom Horn case."

Mr. Marble, wearing an ill-fitting suit, stuck his hand out to Angus. Angus knew what he'd feel just from looking at the man's slouch and the disinterested look on his face. He was what people call wopple-jawed because his lower jaw projected out from his face. He looked uncomfortable.

Angus took the man's hand and resisted the temptation to crunch it. "You're a detective, are you, with the Pinkertons? You're interested in the Tommy George case, are you?"

"No sir, I am not. My work takes place mainly in Illinois, Chicago actually, but I'm on assignment to Denver. The Pinkerton Agency has assignments in cattle rustling in all western territories, and I'm engaged to follow the Thomas Horn case, which I understand is why you too are here from another state."

"I was interested in the Horn case, but now I'm more interested in the ambush of Tommy George."

LeFors took Mr. Marble by the elbow, saying, "Gentlemen, let's go over there to that bench Angus has his bedroll and saddle bags on, shall we?

"Angus, we had words I regret on our last telephone call. I am sorry for upsetting you and hope you'll accept my apology. May I be so bold as to ask where you stand on the Tom Horn case."

"You bet, Joe. I can give it to you straight up. I think Willie Nickel was shot by mistake. The rock under his head was on purpose—to give you a wrong lead. Like moving a horse from a walk to full gallop without trotting or loping. I am suspect about the truth of Horn's confession. But maybe now that doesn't matter. Like I told you on the phone, I'm looking hard at the sum bitch who shot Tommy George."

LeFors asked the ten-dollar question. "Do you think the shooting of Willie Nickel is connected in any to the shooting of Tommy George?"

"No," Angus said. "Ain't got time to explain it, but one's a shooting arising out of a range war between cattlemen and sheepmen. The other is personal and does not involve rustling, cows, sheep, or range detectives. They bear no connection whatsoever."

Ten minutes later, after Angus identified the man he was after and had given them a roundup of what he'd learned in the past day and a half, Le Fors took a different attitude about both cases.

"Angus, you're here in Wyoming at the direction of the Colorado attorney general and the U.S. marshal in Denver. And I welcomed your work in my own office. But that was about the Tom Horn case. You have no authority in the Tommy George case, but I've talked to Sheriff Smalley right here in Laramie City. He wants to deputize you as a nonpaid Laramie County Sheriff's deputy limited to the George case. It's a Laramie County crime, but all sheriffs in Wyoming work together. The rustlers, killers, and such rarely hang around after they do their dastardly deeds. He told me on the telephone yesterday that you're headed up to Casper. That's a smart move. Go on up there. Find the sum bitch you say killed Tommy George and arrest him on the authority of Laramie County and my own office with the U.S. Marshals office in Cheyenne. Can we shake on that?"

They did. Angus got on the train.

CHAPTER 18

ANGUS FOUND A NEW reason to dislike train travel on this trip. This train had facing seats on the next-to-last passenger cabin, and he chose a seat across from a short man with an oversized mustache who would just not stop talking about himself, the goods he sold, Wyoming, and their destination city, Casper.

"Sir, by the look of you I'd say you are a man of the horse, the gun, and I hope of God," the man said after Angus pitched his bedroll and saddlebags in the bin above the seats.

"Two out of three," Angus said. Later he decided that was his first mistake—recognizing the existence of a man who sold tools, kitchenware, pills, and potions of every which kind. When he wasn't selling, he was talking. Only good thing was he took Angus's mind off the irritating rocking sideways motion he hated in trains.

In the first monologue, the man explained the nuts and bolts of Casper. "Did you know, sir, that Casper was named after a military man whose name was actually Caspar, but the U.S. Army misspelled his name on his death certificate? No, I take it by your silence you did not. Well, let me tell you, sir, that your first visit to Casper will be a thrill because the town is seated some five thousand feet above sea level but on the mighty banks of the North Platte River, a river of some standing in a land hungry for water. And it's fitting we're traveling there together on two iron rails because Casper came into being entirely because it was the terminus of one of the first railroads in northeastern Wyoming—it was none other than the Fremont, Elkhorn & Missouri Valley Railroad. They pounded the last stake in the ties in June 1888, just fourteen years ago."

Angus was certain that if he didn't say something, the man would talk about selling long handle shovels to shoemakers, just to prove how good at selling he was. So he asked a question.

"You know a lot about Casper, do you? I hear it's a town where a man can avoid the long arm of the law as long as he's got a stake and keeps to himself. You know anything about cattle rustlers, sheep killers, or those who enforce the law north of the Colorado border?"

"I'm afraid you take me for another sort of man, sir. I have read about such men and I can confirm Casper is an important shipping point for cattle and wool. Are you referring to the terrible goings-on that afflicted a county not too far from here? It was Johnson County. Not that long ago there was upheaval and killing. As I remember the history from reliable newspapers all the way from Cheyenne, it was a time when the beef cattle business was much astir, much astir, as I understand it. Cattle prices went down about twenty years ago. I'm told the reason was the ranges were overstocked and then, of course, there was that terrible drought in 1886 and an even more terrible winter that year. My own father said the cattle business was nearly wiped out."

Angus tried to change the subject. "So your father was a cattleman, was he? How come you got in the home goods business if you grew up riding fence and chasing cows?"

"Oh no, my good man, my father sold fencing materials out of his store in Nebraska. That's how he knew the cattle business."

To avoid any more talk, Angus excused himself to go to the privy in the caboose car. He came back twenty minutes later and hardly got back into his seat when the man renewed the one-sided conversation. But this time it was about something Angus was keen to hear.

"Well, sir, as we were discussing, cattlemen up here, as well as down there on the Colorado border, began publicly blaming their woes on rustlers. And that led to the notion that they had to rid Wyoming of cattle thieves. They went so far as to lynch homesteaders Ella Watson and Jim Averell on the Sweetwater River in 1889. That, my good man, was the event that led to the Wyoming Stock Growers Association engaging a private army of some said more than fifty armed men into Johnson County. Let me see now, yes I have it. It was 1892, just ten years ago. They murdered two rustlers but nothing was done about it."

Angus took a new interest in the peddler. "Lynching and murdering, was it? All over cattle thieving? Don't suppose you know much about the Tom Horn case, do you?"

"Well, my goodness me! Of course I do. Well, I don't know him personally but the papers here and everywhere have been talking about it for a year, maybe more. He murdered a sixteen-year-old boy in Cheyenne, didn't he?"

"No, but there was a fourteen-year old boy killed north of Laramie and Tom Horn will be tried for it come October this year. I looked into his case down there."

"Well, sir, this is then indeed a fortuitous meeting. May I ask the nature of your knowledge of the trial?"

"Nope," Angus said, "but if you know something about Mr. Horn in this part of the Wyoming Territory, I'd be willing to listen to that."

"Happy to oblige. As you have astutely suspected, I'm an avid reader of the news. If my memory serves, there was news about your Mr. Tom Horn just after the Johnson County invasion in 1892—you know, the fifty men I told you about."

"Yes, I believe you did guess it was fifty men."

"Well, sir, after that, the cattlemen were seriously opposed, for market share, by sheepmen. They brought their flocks to ranges cattlemen had long thought of as their own. On their side of the fence, the cattlemen hung to the notion rustlers were the cause of their woes. That's how Tom Horn entered the fray. Did you know, my good man, that a former deputy U.S. marshal, name of Joe Rankin, deputized Mr. Horn to investigate a murder in the aftermath of the Johnson County invasion? He thought Horn had earlier been an agent for the Pinkertons down in Colorado."

Finally, while the man was in mid-sentence, the engineer blew the whistle as they rounded the curved track into Casper. Angus was the first man off the train.

It was dark at the station given it was approaching midnight. Angus could see what he was sure was the middle of the town about fifty yards away. While the mustached little man was irritating, he'd also given Angus a short list of Casper's claims to be an up-and-coming Wyoming city. It had, the man revealed, its own power plant, alongside a small oil refinery, and by-God electric lights from the Casper Electric Company.

"Damned if they don't" he insisted when Angus implied it was more boast than toast. "And we have telephone service since spring. Rocky Mountain Bell Telephone installed forty-nine telephones."

Angus had thanked him for that and said he planned on using one of them first thing tomorrow. The first hotel he came to was a two-story wood-sided building called The Quebec. The front door was unlocked and there was a light on over the chest-high registration desk. Angus found a handwritten note.

"You are welcome to move into the communal room— first door on the right—it has four beds and three are empty. Take one and bring us two dollars fifty in the morning. Breakfast is at seven every morning."

Turned out to be a right comfortable mattress. The pillow had a smell on it. So he used his bedroll for a pillow, laid his Winchester .30-40 under the bed, and stuck his Colt under the tarp. Breakfast was not ready at seven, but the coffee was hot on a little woodstove in the corner. The five-table dining room had four empty tables. He picked one and waited for the cook to come through the kitchen door. The two men on the opposite side had their backs to him. So he sipped his coffee

out of a heavy ceramic cup. No sooner had he got comfortable
at the table for four when one man across the room turned
back to look at him. He wore a black, well-dusted felt on his
head and a five-point star on his leather vest.

"Morning, stranger," he said from across the room.

"Morning," Angus replied, relieved to see he wasn't a
salesman.

"You wouldn't be a deputy sheriff from Laramie County,
would you?" the man said amiably.

"You bet," Angus said, pushing away from his table and
standing toward the man who was slower getting up from his.

"Yep, figured you was. I'm Allan Connell, Natrona County
Sheriff. I got a telephone call late yesterday about you. Johnny
Smalley is not only my friend and fellow sheriff down in
Laramie; he's married to my first cousin, so we're family. He
said you were upright and I could take your word. Come on
over here and meet my deputy."

Sheriff Connell looked like he might have posed for a
Wild West banner. He had that ramrod look that suggested he
could sit a horse and folks would say he was agile enough to
be part horse himself. His handshake was tight, and he didn't
let go easily. His spurs were a little spattered, but the straps
gleamed of fresh oil. What surprised Angus a little was the
rifle leaning against the wall next to their table. It looked like
a .45-70 single-shot Springfield.

"Sheriff, is that what I think it is?" Angus said, pointing
to rifle. "From what I can see I'd say it's a .45-70 single-shot
Springfield."

"Angus," Sheriff Connell said with a smile, "the old gun-smiths around here call it a 'trapdoor' rifle; just one shot at a time. You must know your guns. It is what you think."

"Well, to tell you the truth, most of what I know about guns comes from my wife—she's a gun smith. She has one and I know it packs one hell of a wallop at long range."

Over ham and eggs, the three men talked horses, chases they'd had, and on-the-hoof beef prices in Natrona County. Once the dishes were cleared, Sheriff Connell said, "Let's go to the jail where we can talk about how we can help you find this runaway Crow name of Jean Louis Esme."

Surprised, Angus said, "You sound like you got a lead already. I take it Sheriff Smalley gave you the picture."

"Picture? No we ain't got a picture yet, but I wired the Mounted Police in Calgary yesterday afternoon asking for the particulars on the man you're huntin'. We outta get a reply back sometime today. We have good relations with the Canadians, and they keep records a damn site better 'n we do. Hell, we're primitive compared to how they track and jail thieves and killers in Canada."

When they got to the jail, Angus realized they meant jail. Most often a county sheriff has an office in the county seat with a jail either attached or close by. This was a lot of jail and only a little office. This stone building was narrow, without windows, and fifty feet of barred cells attached to maybe fifteen feet square for an office. From the street, you walked into the twelve-by-fifteen office, and the first thing you saw was a thirty-foot-long hallway containing a big ten-man cell with no bunks, two tables, and benches to sleep on. There were four two-man cells with beds and tables in each. At the far end, in plain sight, was an open privy with two visible toilets, two sinks, and no window. Off to the left side of the door, once you got inside, you'd see the front office. An open door on the far wall looked like a private privy. They assured him their privy smelled better than the one the prisoners used down the hall.

"We only shut the hallway door," Sheriff Connell said, "when we're talking about drunks, pickpockets, sheep herders, or train robbers. Rest of the time, it's left open so we can listen to them bitch about the food coming in, or going out, if you get my drift. Our job is to restrain 'em until the circuit judge stops by every two weeks. He lets 'em go if they only stole to feed a family. If he thinks they committed a bigger crime he sentences them to several years in prison and puts them on the next train south down to Cheyenne where they have a hellava penitentiary, not just a smelly jail like this one."

Angus asked, "What about rustlers? You arrest them too, don't you?"

"Well, you see, rustlers get special treatment and it don't come from us. Rustlers have to deal with men like Tom Horn and well-paid stock detectives in Johnson County. Usually they don't make it to jail. The only restraint they know is a rope."

"Sheriff," Angus said, hoping to change the subject, "you mentioned a phone call yesterday . . ."

"Yes sir, we got one. It is strange they gave us a telephone at all, but once it was up and talking, we found out why. This one was supposed to go in the post office two blocks over, but it burnt down to the ground the day the Rocky Mountain Bell man was supposed to install it. So he walked over here on account of we were the only other official office that didn't have one yet. He put it inside that four-foot square room behind a door. It was intended to be a gunroom, but hell, it's just me, and Sonny here. We wear our pistols and keep our rifles at the ready leaning against the wall behind my desk and his table."

"Well, Sheriff, I suppose you could say it's so all your telephone calling can be confidential, like a private booth. The public phone at the post office in Denver is an inside booth, so folks in the lobby don't have to listen to private citizens arguing with government officials on the line."

"All right, Angus, let's hear your needs in the way of chasing down a low-down murdering Crow Indian."

Angus gave the same short version he'd given Joe LeFors.

"What makes you think he headed this way when he lit out from Laramie County?"

"Well, the way I figure it, there's nothing for him south, east, or west of Laramie County. He's got to have help somewhere, and he can't rely on his half-sister anymore. Can't see him going all the way to Canada because he's known up there. He's half-Indian. He'll find company with tribes in northwest Wyoming and a good part of Montana. But he has to get far enough away from Laramie County where his killing took place, and he has to do it on one horse, with limited provisions on the way. He needs to find a town where he can provision himself and maybe hook up with somebody else who wants to stay shy of the law. There are good trails that follow the railroad and lots of water and grass for his horse. But that horse is gonna give out after a hundred-mile run. Casper looked to me like a logical place for him to head for. I was lucky to get a train ride three days after he killed Tommy George. I figure that maybe he's made contact with someone you might know of in this part of the state. Who up here would help him?"

"Damn, Angus. Sounds like you know Indians and their nefarious ways. Treacherous bastards all of 'em, I always say. And a breed is worse than your average Indian. They got white blood to make 'em smart and Indian blood to make 'em treacherous. He could be hard to catch and will be gunning for you once you line him out. I'd advise plugging him at first sight."

"Well, that's not my way, Sheriff, and anyhow I have no idea what the man looks like."

"Might not be your way, but it's the way we been dealing with breeds that kill white men for a long time. You just said the killing was in Laramie County. Did Sheriff Smalley give you his history lesson about his county?"

"Can't say that he did. We had a short time to talk."

"Here's the short version," Sheriff Connell said. "He's proud to hold that sheriff's badge because a good while back, say back in 1867 I think he said, Wyoming was under the Dakota Territory. We weren't even our own territory. That's the year, according to Sheriff Smalley, who fancies himself a gun-toting historian, when the United States Congress allowed us to be a territory under law. It had only one county—Laramie County. So its sheriff was sheriff of the whole Goddamned thing. Now of course we have law in a dozen counties, but Johnny Smalley says it all started with him, or one of his kin. We became a state just a few years ago, you know that, right?"

"Sheriff Connell, I always appreciate knowing the history of a new state. But I'm out of my usual huntin' grounds. Don't know where to start looking, other than I figured he come here or near here on his way to Montana. I know what to do with him if I catch him—I'll rope him up and bring him in to your hallway jail. You have any direction for me on finding him?"

"Expect we'll be able to help you there. The Mounted Police are mighty good when it comes to documenting the crimes of Indians and other killers. I asked them by phone yesterday to get back to me by telegram. Sometimes they send wanted posters and the like on the train. There will be a train here tomorrow from Calgary. Well, actually it's from Billings. The Canadian connection drops down there every other day. By week's end, we might know what this breed looks like—you know his particulars about height, weight, skin marks. You know some of those damn Indians pierce their ears and brand themselves. Full Indians or half-breeds—don't matter—they are uncivilized heathens, the lot of 'em. If the man you're chasing is a breed, and he killed your friend, he'll hang for it. You can count on that up here in Casper, and I expect down in Laramie too. Now I'm thinkin' about our local lawbreakers. They might hide your breed out. He'd have to pay, but they all steal, you know."

"What I need is a good livery stable. I need a horse. Mr. Jean Louis is not going to ride into town for provisions. If I'm right and he's headed this way, he'll look for provisions and places to hide out. Where in this part of Wyoming might he take refuge? If it was Colorado, I'd be looking at Brown's Hole. Now as to talk of lynching or the habits of Indians, I don't cotton to lynching or anything except a lawful trial."

Sheriff Connell tightened his jaw at the rebuke, but then said, "There's a reliable livery stable across the tracks from the train station. Tell 'em I sent you. They'll outfit you."

The quiet deputy spoke up. "I'd suggest Elkhorn Creek. It runs through Casper Mountain about fifteen miles south. It was sacred Indian country for a long time, centuries maybe.

And a lot of trading, hunting, and fishing up there. A man on the run could find friends there if he knows where to look. They've been hiding stolen beef along that creek for years. It's not particularly safe for single travelers riding through, or women of any kind."

"What's the terrain?"

"You got ten miles of prairie to get there and then a steep climb up over nine thousand feet. It's elk country for sure. The Elkhorn Creek runs about half way up on the western slope of the mountain. At the top, there's no trees and a wind that could pick you up and shoot you smack into the North Platte. Stick an extra blanket in your bedroll."

"Would you say it has high mountain ridges where a man can lose himself from civilization?" Angus asked.

"Sure 'n hell you can. Main reason I know it is, I love riding those ridges myself. But it's no place for a young horse or one that's shy of wind and rain. You'll see what I mean if you go there. And outlaws of all kinds have been avoiding the law there as long as I've been a deputy."

"How long is that?" Angus asked.

"Three years and a day, tomorrow," the freckle-faced deputy said.

Angus walked down to the livery stable and asked the short man wearing coveralls and carrying a hay rake who he needed to talk to about renting a horse for a week or two.

"Me," he said.

"Well, I need a stout animal, with a good head, well shod, and muscled up enough to climb shale and breathe easy at nine thousand feet."

"Gelding or mare?" the man asked, as he kept walking from the hay cart to the open barn.

"Don't matter as long the mare is not in heat this week."

"Mares in heat are in stalls. I got six others that might suit you in the open pen behind the barn. Go take a look and then I'll tell you about your choice."

Angus spotted a red roan with the look of a working cattle horse—well disciplined, steady, and collected. The livery stable who had not identified himself by name said the gelded roan was about thirteen and had been brought in from a big spread in Montana selling horses because the cattle business was dying. He liked him right off because he nickered at him before he led him out of the pen. He picked a wide, swell-forked, double-rigged saddle that looked well used. The liveryman said it was a Montana Great Plains saddle. He picked a bridle, spur bit, headstall reins, two saddle blankets, and a breast collar. Angus asked if he'd throw in a rope, and how much did he wanted for a two-week rental?

"Well, cowboy," he said, "if you were boarding him with me I'd charge you a dollar fifty a day for feed, water, extra grain, and rubbing down once a day. If you take this nimble horse up Casper Mountain, let's say twenty dollars for two weeks and a wanted poster on the board at the jail if you don't bring him back."

Angus turned his coat flap aside to show him his deputy's badge. "Oh," said the man. "You're the law. It's still twenty bucks, but I promise not to ask Sheriff Connell to make a poster of you stealing my horse."

"You bet," Angus, said. "I'll need a gunny sack of sweet grain and an extra water bag. How about twenty-two bucks for the extras and you hold off on the wanted poster if I'm overdue."

CHAPTER 19

ANGUS LEFT CASPER THE next morning not long after sunrise. He was surprised how steady the roan was as they picked their way across the North Platte and headed due south to Casper Mountain. It was clearly visible and Angus realized as they rode closer why it might attract cattle thieves—it had good water and excellent visibility from its lower slopes of anything headed their way from the north.

By midday he was on the first set of switchback trails up the western slope. Two miles up he found Elkhorn Creek. He dismounted there, let the roan cool his feet in the stream, and studied the paper map the deputy had secured for him.

"It's the sheriff's copy," he'd explained, "so try not to get it wet while you're headed up the mountain. It rains up there a good bit now that summer's on its way out. The nights up there are always cold, down in the low forties," he said.

By the time the sun dropped below the western horizon five hours later, Angus had found a sharp bend in the creek with a rock cliff on one side and a pine studded flat area on the upside of the creek. Dismounting, he realized how visible he must have been for the last few hours crisscrossing back and forth as he headed up the creek. He also had a good view of the town and some farmland around it. He could see the North Platte and the railroad bridge across it.

He wished he'd thought to borrow a pair of binoculars. There was a lot to see from up here. Now he realized anyone up here could have had him in site for hours. He made camp, rocked up a small circle for a nighttime flame, and ate a cold dinner of cured pork, bread chunks, and canned peaches.

The nighttime sounds were the same as every other mountain he'd ridden the last forty years. He was always surprised by listening to wind at night. He never paid much attention to how it sounded in daylight, especially when he was horseback. But at night, with his horse tied to a tree close by, he could hear every slip of wind creaking through branches above him and bushes beside him. Tree trunks seemed to open and close. He imagined he could hear unseen wings and twigs falling to the grown softly just a few feet away from his bedroll. And then there was the skunk who he heard crawling toward him during the night and scratching at the end of the tarp over his feet.

You never heard coyote calls, foxes yipping, or wolves howling close to town. But up here, those sounds were like men talking at tables in a busy saloon. Mountain chatter. You just had to quiet yourself and your horse and listen.

Just before false dawn, he thought he heard a much heavier chunking in the brush on the other side of the creek. Bear, he thought. He stood up and heaved a short branch across the creek. But nothing moved. He rolled out from under his tarp and started a little fire for his breakfast coffee.

Long before he could actually see the rising sun on the other side of the mountain, he was riding up the creek looking for sign that anyone else had traveled either up or down this creek. He rode out of a large stand of trees and discovered a long flat area that turned back toward the north side of the mountain toward Casper. Surprisingly, the Elkhorn Creek bed seemed to head that way. He followed it for four or five miles and was amazed to find a wagon road on the eastern side of the mountain. It looked to be a logging road, used to cut thirty-foot-tall Ponderosa pines at the eight-thousand-foot level. So he took it down rather than up toward what looked like a meadow on the side of the mountain.

The campfire smoke was the first sign he wasn't alone up here. He could see it over the tops of a large stand of what looked like Douglas fir. As he got to about a mile from the smoke, the roan pushed his ears up and snorted. There was something ahead on the road he didn't like. Angus neck reined his horse off the road and into the trees as he pulled his rifle out of the scabbard. In the distance he thought he heard the sounds of an axe slicing into a tree stump. Then he heard another sound, one you never hear on a mountain unless another man is close by—a mule braying and a second one responding.

Sometimes mustangs come up this high looking for sweet grass and running water. But mules were farm animals and were never far from their owners. He dismounted and used a lead rope to tie the horse securely. Then, carefully stepping through deep undergrowth, he walked slowly to the edge of the big stand of trees.

It was a sight he'd only seen once before in his life—a giant wagon, eight-feet tall and fifteen long, with a wood top and plank sidings. She was there, not on the wagon seat this time, but standing at the far end of the wagon tongue, watching the valley below. Marguerite Esme in the flesh. She was standing sidewise from him, with her arms outstretched, scanning left to right and back again and looking down at the big plain he'd ridden up the mountain the day before. Casper and the North Platte were visible in the morning haze.

He backtracked, untied his horse, and sucked up a deep breath. Cinching the saddle up a notch, he stuck his rifle back in the scabbard and loosened the leather string tie over the hammer on his Colt. Then he mounted up and took a handful of reins with his left hand, nudging the roan to the edge of the forest. When he got to a spot where he would be visible from the wagon, he put the spurs to the horse and thundered down the slope toward her.

The run to the wagon was a good two hundred yards. But his horse was fresh and got within forty yards of the wagon before she reacted. As he got within hearing range, she ran to the wagon seat and was climbing up to the seat. He drew his Colt and fired two shots in the air. She stopped and turned back to him, leveling her binoculars at him. She climbed down and faced him as he slid the big horse to a hard stop in front of her. Jumping off the spinning horse, he walked the last twenty yards to her with the big Colt barrel stiff-armed out in front of him, and at her.

"Don't Goddamned move or I'll shoot you dead where you stand. Where 'n hell is that no-good bastard brother of yours?"

"Monsieur Angus. So you have found me. I knew you would, but not so soon."

"Quit your jabbering. I'm here for him, not you. Is he in the wagon?"

"Do you see his horse, Angus? No, you do not. He is not here. He was up here, hiding, like the boy he once was. I looked for him in town and a Chinese woman told me he might be up here. *Por favor,* let me explain something to you?"

"Explain? That's what you want to do?" Angus said holstering his gun.

"I do."

Angus tied his horse to the rear of the wagon while Marguerite settled herself on a log near her campfire.

"Do you have that little bottle of brandy with you?" she asked.

"I do. Why do you want a drink this time of day?" he answered.

"Not for me, Monsieur, for yourself. What I have to tell you will not please you."

"Goddamn it to hell. You're confounding me again. How long has he been gone?"

"He rode off day before yesterday. He has a new suit, a brown derby hat, black shoes, not boots, and a large bandage over his nose down on top of his lip. He is cleanly shaven and looks like a town person. By tomorrow morning he will be on a train from Powder River. He is going to Vancouver Island in Canada. You cannot catch him."

*   *   *

"I can catch him, Miss, and when I do your killer brother will face justice in Laramie County for the murder of Tommy George."

"And you, Angus, you're not a killer? You're just a law-man? You know what they would do to him if they had caught him in Laramie or anywhere in Wyoming. They might have tricked him. They might say he confessed, just like they say Tom Horn confessed. He would get the death penalty just like Tom Horn will get. He was a man who maybe deserves to die for other killings. When for you does killing stop? I beg you. Let it stop here. Let my brother die in a leper colony, not at the end of a Wyoming rope."

Angus got up, walked around to his horse, and fished the pint out of his saddlebag. He took a swig and went back with it outstretched to her. She shook her head.

"*Merci*, Monsieur Angus. I do not need to settle myself. I did that when I saw my brother for the last time as he rode down this mountain. He is going to D'Arcy, a place neither of us would go even to catch him. Do you know about D'Arcy?"

"Dee Arecee? Is that a town in Montana? That's your brother's home ground isn't it, Montana?"

"No. D'Arcy is a small island near the city of Victoria, Canada. It is where Chinese lepers live and die. That's where he's going. No one will go there except people who cannot live with themselves. The lepers die in misery in places like that. Jean Louis thinks justice will restore him there. He will suffer not the rope, but the plague. Before he dies he believes he can do justice to himself by helping others. Do you know about restorative justice, Monsieur Angus?"

"I been on the catching end of justice a long time, but not on the court end. I'm not a judge so I don't hand out justice. I ought to tell you that I have not the slightest notion of what you're talking about. Restorative justice?"

Marguerite took a deep breath, blinking her eyes and rolling her shoulders from side to side. "I will try to give you a notion. Restorative justice is a new way of looking at crime. It sees crime and harm in any form as a violation of people and relationships rather than as solely a violation of law."

"I'd say that's a mouthful. Is that you talking or your brother?"

"Neither, actually. A woman wrote about restorative justice a year ago. My brother found it in a letter she wrote to a newspaper in California. Her name was Rebecca Fontaine."

"Well good for her, but I never heard prosecutors or defense lawyers talk like that."

"Neither do judges, Angus. They just follow the law of killing—if you kill another man, justice will kill you. It does not bring back the dead; it only causes more death. Restorative justice is, according to my brother, a way of punishing bad men by restoring them to some kind of goodness. I did not know this about my brother, but he once spent some time in a Jesuit monastery, just after they let him out of prison. He said he could not forgive God for what happened to him in prison, so he could not find himself with the Jesuits. But he remembered what they said about justice."

"Like what, forgiving for killing? That isn't justice, it's just forgetting about a dead man and his family. I just found out Tommy has a son, named after him. That boy is coming home and will live on Tommy's ranch because he owns it now."

"That is good to hear, Angus. A boy loses his father but his property is restored to him. Maybe the boy will find his father again, now that he is back home in a place where he grew up. I can tell you that my brother Jean Louis hopes to find peace again with his father, a French Canadian, who died alone."

"Suppose so. But that don't make letting him get away with murder right, does it?"

"Is he getting away with it? Is going to live on a leper colony getting away with anything? Is that restitution to the George family?"

"I'm not saying that. As for restitution, well, the only good thing is Tommy's son coming back to the Bosler area to take up where his father left off. At least one part of the George family is taking up the slack."

"Angus, you are getting part of it. There should be something more than simple justice when a horrific crime has been committed. What my brother did is horrific; I know that. I will grieve for Tommy and Jean Louis as long as I live. But with justice there should be healing. My brother is going to do that: heal the lepers, or at least find food for them. It will kill him just as surely as a hangman's noose would have.

"How can justice be found in the face of genocide, a crime so vast and evil that it defies simple justice? Is there restorative justice beyond retribution and revenge? Must some kind of justice be done before healing can take place?"

Marguerite bit her lip and looked away from him. Then, after holding back a sniffle, she said quietly, "Can you dispense justice, Angus?"

"Well, I can't say it's justice, but I will catch your brother. How far is Powder River from here?" he asked.

"Not sure," she mumbled, looking past him. "Maybe fifty miles."

"What's he riding?"

"I gave him one of my mules because his horse was played out."

"A mule? He's on a mule that's used to hauling your wagon? I see three mules tied to your picket line. How old is the mule you gave him?"

"He is a little old, you know. All my mules are more than twenty years old. But Jean Louis can ride anything with hair. He's an easy keeper and will eat things in a pasture that horses would never touch."

"Do you grain your mules?"

"Yes."

"How long has the mule you gave him been with these other three tied to the picket line?"

"For about seven years."

"Anybody put a saddle on him in the last seven years?"

"No, but he's ridable. He bucked a little when Jean Louis mounted him yesterday."

"Bet he did. And I bet he fought the bit all the way down the mountain. If he dumps your brother between here and Powder River, he'll spin back and head right back here. Mules are like that; they stick with their team."

"No, Monsieur Angus, Jean Louis can handle a mule."

"Yeah, I know a lot of cowboys say that. But if he got dumped he could never catch a mule headed back to the grain sack in the back of your wagon. Which way is Powder River?"

She pointed northeast. He mounted up and spun his horse northwest. He didn't hold her lying against her, and he came on the fat mule's track a quarter mile down the slope, headed northwest.

CHAPTER 20

A NGUS WALKED THE ROAN slowly from one side of the clearing northwest of the big wagon for about five minutes. He spotted the big mule prints headed downslope. Mule, he said to himself. Big feet and stubborn as a flat rock—a mule in a hurry. He spurred the roan into a lope as he tracked Jean Louis in the early morning sun.

The sun was at high noon over the rolling plain west of Casper. Angus was looking for a man on a mule but wasn't surprised when he found the mule without the man. Off to his left, he spotted the coal-black mule just coming out of an arroyo, burdened by an empty saddle and loose reins dragging on both sides. He loosened the rope hanging on his saddle horn and nudged the roan in the direction of the mule. As he twirled the loop twice over his head, the mule caught sight of him and whinnied. He turned a little away from the mule, hoping not to spook him into a run. That didn't work, and the mule moved from a long trot into a stumbling lope.

Now he could see a bedroll hanging half off on the mule's hindquarter and a heavy stretch of white sweat on his chest. So, he tapped his right spur on the roan's belly and galloped toward the mule, now in a runaway headed south. It took a few minutes, but he overtook the worn-out mule and looped it, then dallied the rope around his saddle horn and began slowing the mule down. It took a hundred yards to get the mule to a full stop.

Bringing the roan to a sliding stop, he dismounted, walking the rope line to the mule. He unhitched the saddle girth and pulled the saddle and bedroll off onto the ground. Slowly, while cooing whoa, whoa, son to the mule, he slipped the bridle and bit down onto the prairie. Then he took his noosed rope off and gave the mule a little slap, setting it free.

"All right, you sumbitch," he whispered to the wind blowing at him from the west, "you're afoot and I'm gonna find you from your runaway mule track." A half-hour later he spotted him, hatless and helpless a half mile away.

Angus pulled his Colt and fired two quick shots in the air. They did their job. The hatless man spun around, gave him a long look, and then started running up the hill toward a rock outcropping.

"OK," Angus said, more to himself than the man ahead, "you don't have a belly gun, or you'd have shot back. But do you have a long rifle? One that you rode with across your saddle like the Utes always did down on raiding parties in New Mexico?"

That question was answered a few minutes later when Jean Louis reached the outcropping and raised a long gun in his direction, with both hands, straight up as though it was a flag waving back and forth. Angus dismounted and unsheathed his .30-40 Winchester. Not knowing the roan's training, he looped the reins onto a large clump of desert sage roots and moved ten feet away. He bellied down on the sand, rested the gun barrel across a ten-inch rock, and lined out a shot just to the right of the outcropping. Boom! Then he moved his front sight to the left and fired again. Boom! It worked exactly the way he hoped it would.

Jean Louis stood up with his rifle held high over his head and threw it forward over the outcropping. Then he waved at Angus, signaling his surrender.

Angus slid his long gun back into the saddle sheath and remounted. Slowly walking the roan toward the outcropping, he held his Colt 45 up in the air with his right hand. Ten yards away, Jean Louis stepped out with both hands raised high, looking more like a scared kid than a black-eyed killer.

"So, it is you. My sister said you'd come. She hoped you might listen to her, but I see that you did not. Should I turn around so you don't have to look me in the face as you blow my head off with that Colt .45?"

Angus didn't answer. He dismounted, gun in hand, and faced Jean Louis. When he got an arm's length away, he holstered his gun and slammed his right fist into Jean Louis's face. The man buckled like a rope sliding off a missed steer. As he hit the dirt, he gurgled blood onto his shirtfront. Then, like a lightweight in a heavyweight fight, he struggled to his knees. Wavering in that awkward position, he tried pushing his way up on his hands, using the rock outcropping to regain a standing position.

"I'm sorry I killed your friend, Mister. There's no explaining it. He got my blood up, and I lost my head. Again. Did she tell you I went to prison because I don't think, I just hit. So, hit me again. I deserve it."

Angus pulled the Colt, cocked it, and slowly moved the muzzle to Jean Louis's forehead. He held the gun in place for a few seconds. Jean Louis closed his eyes but made no attempt to resist or even move his head backward.

The standoff ended when Angus holstered the gun and said, "Turn around, sum bitch, hold your hands together out in front. I'm going to get my piggin' string."

Jean Louis complied and Angus walked back to the roan and dug into his saddlebag. Like all working cowboys, Angus kept short pieces of soft but strong rope used to tie cow's feet together for branding or vetting. He found two and used them to tie the man's hands together.

"Sit down," he said. "I'll get my water bag."

He threw the bag and Jean Louis tried to catch it but missed. He was able to pick it up between his legs as he sat on the ground facing Angus. Uncorking the stopper with his teeth, he took a long drink.

"*Merci*, Monsieur Angus. I will do as you say, but my mind wonders if you know what the penalty should be for me. Do you want me hanged for killing your friend? A man who dishonored my sister? Is that your notion of justice, *por forvor*?

Angus didn't answer at first. He remembered the odd phrase this man's sister had used—*restorative justice.*

"Ain't my place or my decision. I'm arresting you for the murder of Tommy George. In cold blood. At ambush. But I didn't see you do it. And I ain't going to bother interrogating you. Your sister says you did it. And you just confessed to it. I'll walk you back to Casper or drag you if I have to. They'll hold you till the law from Laramie County comes up here to get you. What happens after that is no never mind to me. I don't do justice, I just do the arrestin' part."

"With honor, Monsieur, would you take a little time to hear, how did you put it, my 'notion' of justice? It is a notion some Jesuits practice. They say someday Canada will see justice this way."

"Like I said, you can talk all you want. But you're wasting breath. You'd best save it for the lawmen and for the jury when they try you."

Angus went back to his saddlebags and dug out a small oiled sack with jerky and hard biscuits. He gave a piece of each to Jean Louis and sat on a flat rock looking at the man who gobbled the food like a starved man. Jean Louis liked to talk.

Over the next five minutes, Angus listened without responding.

"Restorative justice," Jean Louis said between bites, "looks at the harm caused by just arresting and hanging men for the wrongs they do. The priests think justice should include repairing the harm done, not just killing those who harm. Sometimes, making those who harm part of the healing process helps the innocent people who suffer because of the harm someone else did. They say bad men should stand up for victims and do good things to make up for their harm. A search for healing is genuine justice, they say."

Jean Louis told him the same thing his sister had talked about yesterday. How he hoped to die in a leper's colony in Victoria, Canada. Those lepers had no one to help them. So he'd go there, catch their disease, and die with them. But before he died, he would do good, he said.

"So that's your justice, is it? You die of leprosy instead of the rope?"

"No, I die for what I did in Laramie County, but before that I help miserable people who cannot help themselves. I restore a little justice for the harm I caused. And maybe that helps heal the victims of my killing."

"Well, that's between you and your God. My job is to take you to Casper. It's a forty-mile walk from here, and I ain't putting you on the backside of my horse. It's gonna take us two days. Get on your feet."

Angus looped his rope around Jean Louis's wrist and over the piggin's string and they turned back east toward Casper. That first mile took almost a half hour because Jean Louis kept falling down and the rope didn't help. Angus took his rope off.

"All right. The rope's off. You walk behind like a caboose on the railroad. Jabber all you want, but talking takes breath and that slows us down."

For the next seven hours, until it turned too dark to walk, Jean Louis spoke in a breathless, dry monotone between gasps for breath and coughing from the sand in his throat. He stuttered about his life, his years in prison, his sexual abuse there, and his life in Montana where they saw him as a "breed." Jean Louis gave him a first-hand look at the life of a half-breed with Crow and French blood. Angus never thought much about hatred based on blood, or trampling a man because his skin was red or his voice Frenchie. But it brought back memories of how some New Mexicans felt about the Pueblo tribes up and down the Rio Grande, and the Navajo on the Northwest corner. He remembered how justice was handed out to white ranchers differently than to dark-skinned men and women. And he started thinking about how bad he felt after he watched a legal hanging in Albuquerque twenty years ago.

When they pulled up for the night in a small stand of Aspens on the side of a steep hill, he built a small fire for coffee and beans. After they ate, with Jean Louis's wrists still tied by piggin strings, Angus asked a question he'd asked one other prisoner some twenty years back.

"How 'n hell do you expect me to believe you if I did let you loose to do what you say you'd do? You say you'd go to Canada and help lepers till you got what they have, and then you'd die of what they have. I have no reason to trust you."

Jean Louis looked down between his crossed legs at the dirt.

"You don't have to trust me, Monsieur. You have only to trust yourself. I know from my sister that you are married to a good woman who herself is good with a gun. What if she told you she believed in restorative justice? What if she said it is better to help the victims of crime rather than just killing the criminal? Would you believe her?"

"Hell yes," Angus said. "But you ain't her."

"Did the man I killed have any family?"

"He had a wife who left him and a son who is coming back now to run Tommy's ranch."

"So, Monsieur Angus, let me ask this. They too are victims of what I did. Who else is a victim? My sister is one. If he was your friend, then you too are a victim of what I did. Would the victims, all of them, say I should be hanged? Would some say it might be better to make me die of leprosy while I helped men and women living in misery—making their lives a little bit better while giving up my own? Might they see justice in that?"

"Hell if I know."

"Just so, Monsieur. But if others you respect could see restorative justice as good and hanging only as revenge, then maybe you should trust them."

Angus didn't answer. He just rolled himself into his tarp and let the beginning of darkness cover him like a blanket as he thought about questions he didn't understand and answers he wouldn't give.

Sometime later that night, Jean Louis fell into the kind of exhausted sleep that makes you numb to whatever else is going on around you. When he woke up just as the false dawn inched up into the eastern sky, he looked across the fire pit. Angus was gone. So was the roan. All they left behind was the water bag and the sack of jerky and biscuits.

CHAPTER 21

T HE LIVERY STABLE OWNER in Casper watched him ride back up to the barn door. "Good to see you back, Marshal. Did you catch your man?"

"No, but it doesn't matter. I like this horse. I'll buy him if you'll trust me to wire you the purchase price. And if you'll throw in the tack and two gunny sacks of sweet grain."

"I can do that, Marshal. He's a fine horse and will probably like your part of Wyoming. Cheyenne, isn't it?"

"No sir, it's not. I've had my fill of Cheyenne and a man named Tom Horn. I'm headed to the western slope of the Rocky Mountains from here down to Durango, Colorado. I'll take a left turn from there and be home in Chama, New Mexico, in a week or two."

Angus rode the ridges all the way, avoiding towns, people, and questions. But he managed thirty-five miles a day and reached Chama in two and a half weeks. He and Jill spent a week talking about American justice. It wasn't restorative and it didn't do much for victims. It didn't prevent killing. It was revenge without healing.

After thinking it over and listening to Jill, he wrote a long letter to Marshal Ramsey in Denver. He didn't mention the Tommy George murder but he did give his old friend his take on Tom Horn's confession. The controversy he described was not about who killed Willie Nickell. For Angus, the controversy was whether Tom Horn confessed to it. He put it firmly—he did not—he could not—because it wasn't true. And because it was a tricked confession, so was the trial. And as Angus saw it, justice was not served—Willie Nickell's family was not served.

Tom Horn was convicted by a jury of Willie Nickell's murder, based on his confession and the widely held belief he was a range detective who killed rustlers for money. The Wyoming Supreme Court upheld the jurors' verdict and the state hung him in 1903. Angus never mentioned the Tommy George case because he took it on himself to investigate. And because he did not think justice was served in the Willie Nickell case, he doubted it would be served in the Tommy George case. In both cases, the controversy was more about who the killer was rather than whether he actually committed the crime. Tom Horn was a hired killer. Jean Louis Esme was a half-breed. Angus came to believe that neither would get a fair trial because of "who" they were rather than "what" they did. He never fully accepted the notion of restorative justice. Aw hell, he thought, I can't fix the ending of anything. Maybe I should just do the best I can here in New Mexico with Jill. Wyoming can take care of itself.

The End